home is like a different time

home is like a different time
eva moreda
translated from galician by craig patterson

Francis
Boutle
Publishers

First English translation published by
Francis Boutle Publishers
272 Alexandra Park Road
London N22 7BG
Tel/Fax: (020) 8889 8087
Email: info@francisboutle.co.uk
www.francisboutle.co.uk

First published in Galician by
Ediçións Xerais de Galicia
Doutor Marañón, 12, 36211 VIGO

A Veiga é como un tempo distinto © Eva Moreda, 2011
Home is Like a Different Time © translation by Craig Patterson
2019

ISBN 978 1 9999037 4 9

This book has been selected to receive financial assistance from English
PEN's "PEN Translates" programme, supported by Arts Council England.
English PEN exists to promote literature and our understanding of it, to
uphold writers' freedoms around the world, to campaign against the
persecution and imprisonment of writers for stating their views, and to
promote the friendly co-operation of writers and the free exchange of ideas.
www.englishpen.org

Introduction

I wrote *Home is Like a Different Time* in the seven months that followed my move to London proper (after three years at a university campus in Surrey) in October 2009. Within a three-mile radius of my new home, I soon discovered, were the Galician Centre, the Cañada Blanch Spanish School and, next to it, the Galicia restaurant – all footprints of the modest Galician exodus to the capital in the 1960s and 1970s. Galicia has a long tradition of economically motivated migration, but, compared to the initial migratory wave that took tens of thousands of Galicians to Latin America in the decades around 1900, the story of the emigrants who left in the 1960s and 1970s (for Germany, Switzerland and, to a lesser extent, the United Kingdom) is not usually told in such epic tones. In both left- and right-wing imaginaries, these emigrants are portrayed as workers with limited political and social awareness who settled abroad and worked hard, their only concern being to live frugally and amass enough savings to return to Galicia (possibly to open a business of their own). They are also assumed to have been thoroughly uninterested in the political and cultural landscapes of their host countries, instead finding solace in a limited, folkloristic view of Galician culture consisting of traditional food, traditional dance and tacky songs by such luminaries as Ana Kiro. It irked me during my years in London – and still does – that a latter wave of Galician emigration, of which I was part, was equally misunderstood by both the right and the left.

It would be pretentious to claim that, when I started writing this novel, I wanted to set the record straight on Galician immigration in the UK, past and present. My aims were considerably less ambitious. I am drawn, as a novelist, towards the creation of fictional universes through words – nothing more, nothing less – and a fictional universe set primarily in that part of London where I now lived, but forty years earlier, sounded like a good place in which to spend some time. I therefore do not claim to be offering a faithful portrait of Galician emigrant life in the 1960s and 1970s, although of course research on the period helped enormously in shaping this universe. So did the scarce precedents in Galician fiction: Carlos Durán's *Galegos de Londres*, Xelís de Toro's *Os saltimbanquis no paraíso* and Xesús Fraga's *A-Z*, as well as his non-fictional accounts of his early life in London as a child of *emigrantes*.

It soon became apparent, in the process of planning the novel, that this fictional universe needed to exist in opposition to something else – and that was A Veiga, the fictional Galician village the characters in the novel come from. It seemed natural that this opposition colonized the characters' relationship with language too: in the original, English words and idioms (and some the language's grammatical structure too) appear interspersed with Galician; these words have been left in English, but italicized, in the translation. If I say that the novel's A Veiga is fictional, this is because the real A Veiga, my birthplace (official name: Vegadeo), is administratively not part of Galicia: it lies on the other side of the border, in the region of

Asturias, although centuries of shared history mean that it is a form of the Galician language (and not Asturian) that is spoken there. The Franco regime and, perhaps even more so, what came next brought an institutional erasure of Galician culture to A Veiga and the surrounding areas in favour of Asturian identity, although things have started to change in recent years. Such intricacies, I decided, probably deserved their own novel; my choice was thus to talk of A Veiga as if it were any Galician village, without drawing attention to its complicated administrative status.

The fictional A Veiga has some resemblance to reality. Like Gelo in the novel, my grandfather, José Ramón Rodríguez Rico, and his mother, Amalia Rico Rico, engaged in *estraperlo* (black market trade) during the 1940s, after their father and husband found himself on the losing side of the Spanish Civil War and was forced to take exile in France. Some in A Veiga emigrated during the 1960s and 1970s; this was the case with my grandfather's older brother, Antonio, a shoemaker like Gelo, although it was in Barcelona where he built a new life for himself and his family.

In the seven years since the novel was published in Galician, it has been hugely rewarding to see first-hand how readers have inhabited, even for a few moments, the universes that I strived to develop in the novel. Readers kind enough to share feedback with me included emigrants and immigrants, present and past, and students of Galician culture at universities outside Galicia, and other individuals with rich and complex intercultural experiences – but also readers who never left the place they were born in; having been an *emigrante* myself for more than thirteen years now, it has often been their perspectives that have struck me the most. I cannot help but hope that this translation by Craig Patterson, generously supported by a PEN Translates Award from the English PEN Club, allows readers in Britain and beyond to do the same.

Eva Moreda
Glasgow 2019

home is like a different time

I wait until the door closes and then get up to make my way back to Croydon in a London slowly being covered by snow. After that, I'm a pale child boarding the train in Veiga with his mother, squeezing her hand when she's afraid, when we're both afraid. I'm that child once again, here, in this country.

Portobello Road

Being afraid began in Portobello Road. Friendship and neglect and surprise and misunderstanding and pleasure too. But all that now remains is being afraid, the feeling that began years ago in Portobello Road.

'Gelo!'

The girl, that Twiggy with dark hair and more abundant in shape than the real Twiggy, but also more extravagant in appearance and so to my eyes much more *chic*, crossed the dance floor towards me as she waved. London, after three weeks, was still a confusing and sometimes embarrassing tide, names here, faces there, which Tino fleetingly introduced and which would then sink once again in the waves made by the city. I remembered that I had noticed her when she came into the bar that evening (she was smoking in a corner with another, similar looking girl) and that I had asked myself what those two confused English girls were doing in our bar, the bar in Portobello Road.

The girl was making her way towards me between the dancers who crowded the floor (*Sugar baby love, sugar baby love*, sang a sweet, masculine voice that had already prompted some ironic comment from the group of men who I had sat down with at the start of the evening). I focused my gaze, and at first it was a spark of lucidity, and then incredulity, and even a certain despair. By that time, the girl had reached me and kissed me on the cheeks.

'It's me. Elisa. The Barreses' Elisa.' She uttered the last part hastily, as if all those old affiliations, nicknames and family names from Veiga were nothing more than meaningless words not worth dwelling upon in London. 'You didn't recognise me, did you? No wonder, with my hair like this! I told Lidia that I didn't want the Nigerian girls to cut it again, but it was the only place I could afford.'

You went on and on and I couldn't help but feign a smile, amid the surprise, for times gone by, before interrupting you.

'Lidia? It's Lidia, right…?'

'Yes. Lidia, the one from Piantón. Look, over there, here she comes.'

Another girl with short hair, this time with a mini-skirt and tight sweater on, appeared behind you, put her chin on your shoulder and her hands festively around your waist. I also recall having seen her at some point in the evening, dancing on the floor with some lad who seemed far less inclined than her to go mad about London trends. I hadn't recognised her, either. I remembered Lidia like a little grey mouse, as thin as a rake (and that's why the Twiggy style in London suited her perfectly, and better than you, if I may say so), always looking at the ground so that nobody would notice her, always hanging on to your tail. I remembered that one summer when I had been in Veiga on holiday, during my Lugo years, I accidentally heard that Nela and Celestino, Lidia's parents, had gone abroad. I knew Nela well: in the toughest years, she had left my mother and me half dozens of eggs by the door for free, when she was going from Piantón to sell her merchandise in the few houses in Veiga that were still well off. But I hadn't thought about her until Lidia was in front of me. Her daughter, on the dance-floor of the bar in Portobello Road.

'We have to get going,' Lidia told you, still holding you by the waist. 'You know what my mum will say if we spend too much time here. And tomorrow at half four…'

'Look, Lidia, it's Gelo. Don't you remember him?' you replied, gesturing with your hand towards me.

'Oh, yes. Hello, Gelo.' Lidia looked at me, but I wasn't sure if she'd really seen me. Her life in Veiga, those quiet boys, badly shaven and badly dressed, who knew nothing about the Beatles, or the Monkees, or Twiggy, lay far behind her now, 'London' Lidia seemed to think as she looked at me vacantly. 'Look love, we've got to get going, or my mum…'

'I'm coming, don't rush me.' And whilst Lidia disappeared again amongst the mass of dancers, you took a serviette from a table, a pencil from your bag, scribbled something and offered me the serviette whilst giving me a quick peck on the cheek. 'Come and see us sometime, right? Call first, if you want. But we're mostly always at home in the evenings. Unless we're out shopping, of course.'

Churchmead Road, Willesden Green, said the piece of paper that you gave me. Back then, I still didn't know where Willesden Green was, but the postcode, which you had written below, began with NW, and I had been in London long enough to know that it meant the *Northwest* of the city. I had heard that a lot of people from back home were living in the north-western suburbs: Notting Hill, Harlesden, Ladbroke Grove. Perhaps Willesden Green too. Also in the south, where NW simply became a W for *West*: Kensington, Victoria. Few lived as far away as I did. The Croydon postcode didn't begin with N, or S, or E or W: Croydon was just CR, and for *born and bred* Croydon people at least, that was no longer London: Mr and Mrs Stobart always said they were from Croydon, just Croydon. All that stuff didn't matter so much to me then. My destination had always been London: it was London and not Croydon where Tino had convinced me to go and find work.

That was little more than three months ago. But when I returned home from Portobello Road, on the train that took me from Victoria to East Croydon, it seemed like three years. London has something which makes everything that doesn't belong to it seem like it was discarded in some attic years beforehand. There, in that attic, my first conversation with Tino, my conversations with you, lay all tangled up, the words woven together. It had been three months since the first. Five years since the second.

Tino would say hello to me every day when he got back from eating at his sister's and found me sat smoking in the doorway of the house in Fondrigo. Alright, how are you, a hasty slap of complicity on the shoulder, until one day he came over to ask:

'How come you're always here? Are you on holiday?'

It wasn't a particularly respectable story and Tino was not and never has been a close friend, but it didn't make much sense to fake a success that neither Veiga or Lugo had brought me, and that now I was getting on for 40, I didn't think any city would. But then, of course, I still didn't know London.

'Nope. The shoe shop in Lugo wasn't doing well and I had to close it. It's not like it ever went well for us, but since Inés died, there was no other way. I had to close it before I got saddled with debts. There was no other way.'

Tino's mouth was wide open; his dark eyes that had once broken so many hearts were now popeyed.

'Inés…?' he said, at last. 'I'm really sorry, I had no idea…'

'No, no, you don't have to say sorry. How were you to know? It was last spring, in April. You weren't here. When you're far away, home is like a different time.'

Tino agreed, his expression becoming alert and regaining that look he had of a second-rate film star, that half smile and teasing gaze that had caused so much bother between mothers and daughters ten or fifteen years ago in Veiga, when I was the same age but not very interested in girls and they weren't very interested in me. To go to London, Hamburg, even Madrid or Barcelona, as some people go, was to really go: to be resigned to not seeing Veiga for a year or two. It was knowing that in your mind, Veiga was going to be frozen in that same moment when you left, and no child would be born or anyone die like Inés had. It was to accept that Veiga is like a different time. Going to Lugo or Coruña was a different thing. You went and came back every month, or every two months, and time kept passing too in Veiga, and people kept dying and being born, as always.

It wasn't like that for me. For me, Veiga had ended up becoming a different time too. From the beginning (the idea to leave had come from her: we didn't need to, not if we didn't have children, as had been the case until then), Inés had wanted to sell the house, the shoe shop. That's how we jumped over the final hurdle that tied us to Veiga after her father died and left me the business. If it hadn't been for that matter of selling the shop, I sat thinking in front of the house in Fondrigo with a half-lit fag between my fingers, I could be mending shoes and earning a living now, with no need to rely on the insincere charity of those unsociable relatives. That's what I told Tino that very afternoon as we had the second or third drink. Tino had invited me to spend the evening "on the piss, like when we were lads", he'd said. I couldn't remember the last time I'd spent an evening that way and accepted the invite without too much protest: I didn't like depending on the generosity of my barely recovered friend, but I needed to escape however I could from that temporary abode.

'*No problem, man!*', Tino replied. 'Do you need work? Come to London!'

'It's not that easy,' I objected. 'I don't speak English. I only know how to mend shoes.'

'That's no problem, I'm telling you. You pick up how to carry a tray in no time. Look, I work in a restaurant and they want to take on a few new waiters in September. Tomorrow I'll write to my boss and tell him about you. He likes to have people from back home working there, and if I recommend you, count on it. He likes people from back home better than Italians: Italians are lazier and complain more. And don't worry about English. I hardly spoke a word when I got there, and look at me now! No English girl can resist me!' Tino roared with laughter as he patted me on the back.

The next day, Tino wrote to his boss. A week later, he received a reply from Mr Stobart. He would be *delighted*, he said, to take on *Mr Martínez* as a waiter, for forty hours a week over six shifts and a wage of fifteen pounds a week. Tino was almost more delighted than me; I was too busy going every morning from the police to the doctor and from the doctor to the town hall and listening to my friend in the evenings: his tales told of rain and bad food and two-storey red buses and the Tube and kind bosses and highly eccentric customers and, above all, English girls who would agree to anything without any objection. And the real reason for his living in London, which he didn't reveal to me until he had me on board for sure.

'A Galician restaurant,' he told me again and again in Barrica's bar that we both now visited everyday (his generosity allowed me to). 'In London, it's the perfect business. Hardly surprising, with how bad their food is! If I told you what you're going to have to serve in *The Two Roses*, if I told you... It's the perfect business. There are many Italian and Greek restaurants over there, but I still haven't seen a Galician one. And they're going to love what we eat. It's the perfect business.'

'But it's going to be difficult to open a restaurant,' I replied. 'If we need all this paperwork to go and work for other people, imagine what it's going be like to start our own business.'

'Nah! Once you get there, it's as easy as pie. I knew a few blokes, a lot dozier than you and me, who opened bars and *off-licences* without any problem.' Then he lowered his voice. 'Over there you don't get that good conduct certificate nonsense, and the Civil Guard, the mayor or the priest have nothing to do with these things. It's different.'

Tino was right. There was none of that. Sat on the train for East Croydon, at Streatham Common, I still found it strange not seeing those green uniforms suddenly get on board, the ones that made my heart miss a beat when Inés and I used to go on the train from Lugo, although it's been a few years, quite a few years since those trips (one way only) on the train to Pontenova. Every time a Civil Guard got on the train, my mother would take me by the hand and squeeze it tight, and I didn't say a thing, even though I was thirteen and holding your mother's hand was for babies.

That train wasn't bound for Pontenova, but East Croydon, although when I looked out of the window, Selhurst slightly resembled Reme. It always did and still does sometimes with these night trains. Lately, when I look out, it seems as if I'm seeing you, although when I take a better look it always turns out to be someone else. That time, that day in Portobello Road, the day when everything began, I didn't make that mistake again until I reached my destination. From East Croydon, I went on to

Davidson Road. It was December and it was snowing: the first time I had seen it snow in London.

Willesden Green

NW, the *North West*. That was your first quarters in London, the winter quarters that now you've abandoned *for good* to disappear, to lose yourself. After Portobello Road, I still took two weeks to take the train northbound, and then the Victoria Line and the Jubilee line towards that place that at that time was still beyond the borders of my London. Willesden Green. There was something magic, exotic and dangerous about the name of that suburb for me. Just over a month after my arrival in London, English was still an immense, dizzying language for me, at times like a tide beyond control (not that it's any different now), and pronouncing "Willesden Green" was just the same. In comparison, Croydon sounded vulgar and plain. When I left the Tube station, I had to acknowledge, as is mostly always the case in London, that the name was deceptive. Willesden Green was no more than a *high street*, like the one back in Veiga, which had sprung up in no time around Irish, Pakistani, Indian, Caribbean and Portuguese businesses. I recalled that Celestino, Lidia's father, had done some of his military service in Africa and had never managed to overcome his aversion to Arab or Black people, and was still talking about them with barely concealed disgust years later in the bars of Veiga.

And then I saw her face / I'm a believer. The Monkees, one of the favourites on Sundays in the bar in Portobello Road, could be heard from the street outside. When Nela, who was older, quite a lot older than I remembered her, opened the door for me, I had to shout to be heard above the chords of the guitar, that sound I was now beginning to get to know and appreciate a little after almost six weeks in London. Before coming to this city, I wasn't too fussy about music. I liked to hear the Veiga band play every Sunday on the stand. I liked to have the radio on whilst I worked alone in the workshop and listen to the dance tunes, as I'm sure everybody does in Veiga. But London is different: people love music here. People seem to need music like the air they breathe.

'Elisa. You've got a visitor!'

I heard a door bang on the other side of the house and you appeared, with your hair wet and wearing a very short shift dress, and no tights on underneath.

'Oh!' you exclaimed. 'We were trying clothes on, trying to sort out this disaster with my hair…' you added as you were drying it. 'How's it going?'

The house in Willesden Green strongly resembled an English house. I for one had never been in an English home (I hadn't been there long enough to get an invitation, and even now I don't receive many: the English don't let you enter their castle so easily), but Tino had been two or three times to the Stobart's house and talked about shelves with weeks' worth of dust on them and forgotten garments lying around everywhere and people (the Stobarts had three teenage children) coming and going and banging doors and leaving cups of tea in the wardrobes or on the stairs. When I pointed out that our flat in Davidson Road, in Croydon, the one we shared with Davide, our friend from Naples, wasn't much better, Tino replied:

'It's not the same. We're three men and clearly a woman's touch is needed. If my girlfriend or one of our sisters came once or twice a week it would be different. We'd sort it out. But that lot aren't bothered. I'm telling you, Mrs Stobart and her daughters are a lot worse than men. I've seen it myself.'

Nela, who I always remember as being serious but smart, always friendly but not much into chit-chat when she had to go and sell eggs or darn trousers around the houses, did not suit that role of a carefree English mother, indulgent and a little detached. Perhaps it was the years that made her that way, because Nela must have been around sixty: when I was still a boy, she had long since become a woman. Back then she had a little girl; Lidia, a late daughter, always spoilt, had come along later at the wrong time.

'Where's Luísa?' asked the woman when I managed to remember the name of her oldest daughter. 'Did she come to London with you too?'

You laughed. If you were in London now, in front of me, leaning against a column, in an outfit that you would never dare to wear in Veiga (you explained, whilst answering Nela), it was precisely because Luísa had decided not to go. These days, at times, I think about how different everything would have been if Luísa had come and you had stayed behind. Luísa wouldn't have thought of disappearing like you did, and it's also true that I wouldn't have looked for Luísa with the same enthusiasm.

Nela and Celestino had been thinking of leaving for some time. They were getting too old for escapades, that was true, but in Piantón they had just lived from one day to the next, and nothing awaiting them anywhere else could be much worse. The daughters were no longer kids, either, but nothing (a job, studies or boyfriend) tied them to Veiga. At the beginning, they thought about Lugo, Madrid, Barcelona. They found it hard to get used to the idea that Veiga could start to be a different time for them. But afterwards, through one of Celestino's relatives, they found out about a family hotel in London, the Waycott Hotel, in Paddington, which was looking for three cleaners. These were going to be, at the very beginning, Nela, Luísa and Lidia. But Luísa, who until then had always been included in the travelling party, said to everyone's surprise that she wasn't going: she had a boyfriend in Veiga and wanted to marry him. That was when you took her place.

At the Waycott Hotel, they still thought that it was Luísa who had come from Veiga to clean and make beds. It wasn't your intention to fool your bosses, you quickly assured me (speaking of permits, passports and papers was always done, and is done, with reverence, almost fear), and your name appeared on your work permit and your contract, but the Waycott family, with the first letter they received through contact with you, already assumed that their new cleaners would be called Manuela, Lidia and Luísa. Or *Louise*. Even your workmates called you that, and Lidia and Nela too when they were with one of them or the Waycotts. And in the house in Willesden Green, I once heard them call you by that name, out of routine, and you always answered them immediately, because you had already begun to be slightly Louise.

I couldn't help smiling when you told me. They re-baptised me too as soon as I got to London. It was my first day at work, when I went to The Two Roses with Tino, who was full of himself for having vouched for me. Tino settled down without a peep between Mr Stobart and me, and the two of us soon began to communicate through him. Everything was going smoothly until Mr Stobart asked for my work permit. He looked at the document in astonishment, opened and closed his eyelids a few times and then uttered a string of words that seemed more indecipherable and threatening than English seemed, in general, on what was barely my first day in London. Tino nodded seriously.

'Is something wrong?' I asked. 'Isn't the permit valid?'

Tino chuckled and Mr Stobart looked at him, puzzled.

'Yes, man, of course it's valid. He's just saying that it's strange that a man's called "Ángel", or *Ayn-gell*, as they say. He doesn't think it's appropriate for him to call you that.'

'Tell him everyone calls me "Gelo". He can call me that.'

That didn't convince Mr Stobart either. It sounded too much like *Hello*, and he argued that I would never know if they were talking to me or greeting somebody else. Finally, he looked silently at the work permit again and said something to Tino.

'He says that he prefers to call you Martin. Well, Martiño. By your surname. I don't think he can pronounce "Martínez" either.'

And so, in the restaurant, I became Martin, and when a new workmate would appear, I got used to introducing myself that way, to avoid adding even more to the confusion that usually prevailed at The Two Roses. As some colleagues left (the oldest, those who were already there when I'd arrived and who I'd told my real name), and others came along, I became more and more Martin and less and less Gelo, and nowadays the regular customers, the ones who have known me for years, call me Martin and can't imagine my real name being anything else, as Gelo was left behind somewhere, in a different time. At the Waycott Hotel, Elisa was more and more Louise and less and less Elisa. And perhaps outside the hotel, too. I didn't like it at all that it was Tino and not me who first noticed it one Sunday afternoon in the bar in Portobello Road.

You and Lidia used to dance with each other (you hardly ever danced with any lad, even though you had no lack of suitors), both dressed in your miniskirts and tight sweaters. Tino had been sitting for a while, looking at you, eyes half-closed and the sixth beer of the evening in his hand. In a critical tone that didn't suit him very well, he suddenly said:

'Of course, with girls like these it's always the same. They come here without knowing anything else about life than the nonsense put in their heads by the Women's Section of the Falange. And here they see a few things, put on a shorter skirt and think they're cleverer. It's the parents' fault, too. They let them get away with every-thing, of course. More than one of them will end up in a pickle'. And he looked intently at you and Lidia.

When I told him that those two girls were from Veiga and that the tallest was a friend of mine, and also pointed out to him that he had changed girlfriends twice in the barely two months I had been in London, Tino replied, laughing sarcastically:

'Mate, that's different. Why can't I enjoy myself a lit-tle? And by the way,' he added, punching my shoulder playfully, 'if that blondie's your friend, it's about time you introduced me to her.'

The life that you and Lidia led from Friday evening to Sunday night, the life that was so hard for me to under-stand, raised suspicions, and not just in Tino. People in Portobello Road thought Nela was a good woman, but didn't understand why she let her daughters out at night (the real and the pretend one, although in London they were more or less the same thing) without a brother, cousin or even a friend of the family with a bit of common sense to protect them. Perhaps it was because in London things matter less. Words (good and bad), looks, setbacks, friendships struck up with someone or another whilst smoking a cigarette or waiting for the bus. Everything is

less important, because London is immense and its borders extend beyond what I and the people I know can
cover (even the English, like Mr and Mrs Stobart, who
only leave Croydon to go into town when then can't
avoid it), and little by little, you become aware that whatever you can or cannot do will in no way influence the
ebb and flow of that immensity, that mass, that gravitat-
ing mass that ended up swallowing you as it twists and
turns, and so everything ends up being less important, less
than in Veiga.

Hardly four months after arriving in London, I was
already becoming infected with that feeling, so how were
you not going to be infected, even intoxicated, you and
Lidia, who both had two years over me? And so, in spite
of the looks Tino gave, those looks from men like Tino
and women who perhaps regretted not being younger or
more daring in following the same road, eventually you
stopped hiding what everybody already suspected every
time you went to Portobello Road.

Lidia was the first to dare. As soon as she went into the
bar in Portobello Road that Sunday, when I had already
been in London more than half a year, it was clear to
everyone that that lanky, gawky lad with the long sym-
metrical hair in the style of The Who that people look at
so suspiciously in Portobello Road, was not one of us.
Now that happens more often. There are a few married
couples and even a couple of kids who are from here and
there at the same time. But when Lidia appeared with
that big lad on her arm and, above all, when she left with
him shortly after arriving without anyone riding shotgun,
we didn't bother to conceal our bewilderment, even our
disgust, and Tino least of all, in spite of Lidia just doing
exactly what she had done time after time since she had
set foot in London.

You still took a few more weeks, but in the end, you appeared with that layabout who studied at University College London and who smoked roll-ups. I still remember him: Graham. Then came Ian and Nick and Luke and even Benjamin, I think. I find it hard to reconstruct those first months in London. During the week, I was trying to unravel the shape of Croydon, of London, like a good student. Then after that in Portobello Road on Sundays: that tide of faces, hands, hair, and you always smiling in the centre like a mistress of ceremonies, like that mysterious *Cheshire cat* that the kids here know so well. The Cheshire cat that vanishes into the air for only its smile to remain: that's you. I find it hard to reconstruct those months because, ironically, what I best recall about you are those interrupted conversations that I had with Lidia every time I didn't see you in Portobello Road. She was usually dancing on the floor or having a beer with her companion, or alone when she was *between boyfriends*. I went over to her, and I felt a little like I did at the dances in Veiga, like when I would go over to the best friends of other girls more than twenty years ago, but Lidia knew very well that we were no longer in Veiga. The dances in London were a lot more frenetic, *busier*, and above all, merciless.

'And what about Elisa?' I asked, trying not to appear too interested. 'I bet she's having a tea with Luke.'

'Oh yeah, a tea.' Lidia exchanged a knowing look with her companion who, as always, didn't understand a thing, and continued dancing or drinking. Or maybe she rolled her eyes and said, 'Luke! Whatever happened to Luke?'

Regarding those months, I recall a sense that everything was changing London. Not even the dances were dances any more, not even friends were who they had been, nor did you girls who had been raised under Miss

Brígida's protection wear a veil on Sundays or a skirt beneath your knees. You were too busy living your own *Summer of love*. And I started to wait for the big change too, the one that would put an end forever to Gelo from Veiga and would create a new Gelo, a London Gelo: sharp, *smart*, slightly impressionable and a little tough, as everybody in that city seemed to be. I waited. And nothing happened. And over time I realised that my initial feeling had not been entirely accurate: really, very few people change other than in a superficial way. We all go on being what we were in Veiga, or in Coruña like Rita, or in Ourense like Dolores or Marta. The same role, with just a different stage, which is why at the beginning we were all a little lost. Very few people changed. Tino's going with one girl after another, but he's still the big conceited lad that I knew over twenty years ago in Veiga. Lidia's going with one lad or another, but she never stopped being the girl who sat in church with her knees together and her head bowed. You did change. But when I saw you in Portobello Road, in Willesden Green, with Graham, with Ian, with Nick, even though you were nothing like the Elisa that I'd once known, you had hardly started to change. You were still barely at the start of that road.

Oxford Street

Liz & Lydia. It seemed like the name of a London singing duo, those pretty little English girls with soft and uneven voices who tried to emulate, without much success, Françoise Hardy, since the option of being the female answer to the Beatles, Stones, Monkees, those groups that the youngsters liked in the bar in Portobello Road (I was a bit old for all that, as you know), didn't seem at all feasible. All the musical training you two had came from Miss Brígida and the choirs and dance troupes of the Women's Section, but in London you'd soon forgotten about all that. In London, that wasn't much more than a small and inconvenient family secret. In London, you were *Liz & Lydia*.

I don't know where that trend came from. English people, you said, always assumed that Elisa came from Elizabeth, and ended up abbreviating it to Liz. And Lidia took to writing her name with a "y". I don't know if you got those things from that string of English boys you met in the pubs and discos of Soho and then took (at least the most worthy and interesting ones) down Portobello Road one Sunday, first to the surprise and then indifference of the locals, because even that became a regular habit, and when the first kids began to be born whose father was from over here or mother from over there, or vice-versa, your English lads no longer caught people's attention.

Liz was the icing on the cake. When you dropped Elisa and Luísa and Louise and used Liz, you already realised that you moved like an English girl, laughed like an English girl, thought like an English girl, even spoke like them, but with your accent. That was, I think now, Elisa's first disappearance, but then I got you back. I got you back like one of those English girls with cream-white hair and a ridiculous little nose who went mad over Mary Quant and Twiggy and spent their days at university desks or at their secretary's table thinking about the moment when the bell would ring and they could break free to take Camden market by storm. Those English girls didn't do the cleaning in glorified guesthouses like the Waycott Hotel. They would hope, at the very least (if they didn't want to go to university or know how to type) to serve customers in the fashion temples of Oxford Street. And that was what you set out to do.

You began to desert Lidia in the afternoon. You would go to the city centre directly from the Waycott Hotel, look in the shop windows in search of advertisements for *Retail assistant wanted*, and if there weren't any, go in and ask the *manager*. Lidia would sometimes complain to me, because that meant she no longer had a friend for her expeditions into Camden Town or the Soho bars. But I said nothing, because the more Lidia's favour decreased, the more mine grew.

It was at that time, and I don't know how, when you took me as a confidant in London. People said nothing, nobody was shocked, not even someone turning their head when they saw the two of us, a man and a woman, having a cup of tea or enjoying a few beers together. In Portobello Road, they gave us funny looks at the beginning, then they got used to it, because in London things are not as important: they are less important. And I found out about all your trips up Oxford Street, down Oxford Street, two miles, *we don't currently have any open positions, sorry but we're looking for someone with better English*, excuses, refusals, sometimes doors closed as soon as they heard your accent, and you, who didn't give up and kept aside two afternoons a week to plan your conquest of Oxford Street, and with it, England. And in between all that I found out more about your boys, because on weekends you still went with Lidia, and that's how I knew about Henry and Ian and Nick, and that's why when I finally found out about Jim, I couldn't avoid feeling a certain relief, because Jim sounded like as if all that coming and going of university students from good families (that's what I supposed, although I never knew: we weren't that close) and Oxbridge or University College was finally going to dry up.

Jim was deputy *personnel* manager at the Marks and Spencer on Oxford Street, the jewel in that street's crown, the most English place where you could work. After weeks handing in *application forms*, they called you for an interview. *Liz*, you had written in the box marked *First name*, and perhaps that, even though your surname didn't fit, made them think that you were a Londoner *born and bred*. Jim had substituted his boss, who was on holiday, on the interview panel, and that's how it all began. Three days later, he called you personally to inform you that you had been taken on, in spite (he didn't tell you that until later on, and you and I found out afterwards) of the reservations of the section manager, who was not sure how the very *middle-class* customers of that establishment would take your imperfect accent, your at times intuitive English. Three days later, after a not very elegant farewell from the Waycott Hotel, you began to work at Marks and Spencer in Oxford Street, the most London establishment in the most London street in London. And just three days later, Jim, James Lawford, *Harrow born and bred*, went over to you on the *Women's clothes* counter to ask about how you were getting on and, in passing, ask you *out*. I learnt all this effortlessly and at first hand. Now I, and not Lidia, was your confident in London. And it didn't hurt me that you said yes to Jim so much as discovering that Elisa from Veiga was now increasingly Liz, and that her outline was gradually fading amongst the tide of shop assistants from Marks and Spencer (*middle-class* English women, not that old and still given to reliving the nocturnal and alcoholic madness of their recent past, but who above all else had made *common sense* their religion), who in those days flooded London. That tide that kept swallowing you up only to spit you back out just as often, but that now seeks to keep you, merciless as London always is, within its depths.

Brighton

Shortly after beginning to go out with Jim, you told me that I needed a girl too. It was one day when the three of us met in a pub in Fitzrovia. Jim didn't like Portobello Road, which is why we had to meet up in a pub in Fitzrovia, Soho, or even West Hampstead, where he had bought his bachelor flat not long before. That was Jim. He was in his country. He liked being there and he could simply not imagine the thought of leaving it, even for just a minute, even when just pretending.

'That way you won't always have to ride shotgun,' you said. 'And the four of us can go to Brighton for a swim on Sundays.'

Colleagues from Marks and Spencer, Italian or Greek girls from Willesden Green, girls who we both knew from Portobello Road: for a while, every time we saw each other, you would speak to me of a potential candidate, and each time you told me that she was perfect for me. I didn't feel that I needed a woman in my London life. On my side, with widowers and old bachelors, I had at first discreetly watched couples get together and split up. Then, very gradually, with increasing naturalness, contaminated perhaps by the *openness* of the English. But I'd never thought that I could be contaminated too. Your assumed role of go-between disconcerted and dismayed me. No, my best friend in London wasn't there for that, shouldn't do that. When you began to insinuate that Lidia, who at that time was, as they would say here, *between boyfriends*, and I wouldn't make such a bad couple, I decided myself to choose the girl who I least disliked. To go with you to Brighton in the summer, to not stop seeing you all those months. I'd have time to think later about what would happen after that.

The one chosen was Rita. Rita had worked for a while in the kitchen of The Two Roses. Like all the rest, she was not immune either to the fascination that Tino seemed to exert (always for a limited period, of course) upon every single woman under forty who started working at the restaurant. Rita was no exception. Shortly after arriving, although with her relationship with Tino now on the wane and then dramatically ended, she handed in her notice and moved to Sutton to cook at the Raymond's house, those old snobs who had always looked at me as if I wasn't there, as if I were not good enough for their cook. Rita still went up the Portobello Road now and again, and had never stopped saying hello. But not to Tino, who she grimaced at every time she saw him appear, jacket over his shoulder, his asymmetric and irresistible smile, with that arrogant posture that made everybody in London look at him strangely.

Rita was actually fleeing from Tino (she would look out of the corner of her eye towards the dancefloor to check that he wasn't following her, which was unlikely, on the other hand, as it seemed that he had found better company) when she unceremoniously bumped into me one Sunday evening in Portobello Road.

'Oh,' muttered Rita. 'Sorry'.

Her podgy cheeks were brighter than usual. The heat, a temperature, embarrassment. She still had the trace of *lemonade* above her lip. I felt sorry for her. *Lovely Rita, Meter Maid*, I though whenever I saw her, and once I even hummed in a low voice that melody that I'd heard so often in my first months in London about that Rita of the Beatles, the parking meter maiden, graceful and pretty in her blue uniform, who so little resembled the Rita from

Coruña that I knew. I felt pity and tenderness towards her.

'Tino again, right?' I asked. Until then we hadn't talked much. There was hardly ever a chance in the restaurant: customers, more customers, half-yelled orders, plates that smashed and, almost always, Mr Stobart in the middle trying in vain to make himself heard above the racket. And Tino always liked to keep his *affairs* separate from his domestic life with Davide and me.

She nodded quietly like a girl whose mischief has been interrupted.

'Don't say anything to him, alright?' she replied.

I also nodded with pretend solemnity. Clumsy as she was, Rita would always break a glass or pull down a curtain every time she put into action one of her escapes after seeing Tino. It was difficult for everyone (as well as for the person in question) not to notice.

'Fancy a cup of tea?' I asked.

She agreed, relieved. Her mouth was dry and her pulse racing from the flight, but it was nothing that a cup of tea with milk and *two sugars* couldn't solve. Tea sorts everything out, as you know, although I never really ended up liking it. Antonio, the pub manager, who was at the bar, seemed surprised that we ordered tea, or, perhaps, what surprised him was seeing me sit down with Rita, who always ended up dancing alone or with another of her single friends, but he didn't say anything. He put two cups in front of us of *English Breakfast* that he kept for when some clueless English person appeared in the pub, a little jug of milk and a few somewhat extravagant olives for the right moment and situation, and then went off to see what they wanted on the other side of the bar. Rita's cheeks were still blushing, but now she was smiling and sat with her legs crossed and elbows resting with a certain elegance on the bar. And I noticed that in spite of her outfit being a greyish colour that was not very attractive to the eye (and which of course would suit a sixty-year old woman better than a thirtysomething), it was an elegant cut and not the worst of its kind. It seemed like Rita wasn't doing too badly at all with those old people who she cooked for in Sutton.

'Not many men invite me to have tea, you know?' and she said it as if she were apologising for her clumsiness, but she added the start of a coquettish little giggle at the end. I tried to feign surprise: after all, I was only offering a tea to an old friend who was hot and bothered, wasn't I? No, not exactly, and I knew it. Almost from the moment when Rita had looked at me with those eyes like a stunned calf after I bumped into her chest, I began to ask myself what it would be like to take Rita to Brighton, and to introduce her to you and Jim, for the four of us to spend Sunday evenings lying on Brighton beach now the good weather was on its way and we didn't fancy staying indoors in Portobello Road so much. I didn't dislike the idea.

That night I went with Rita to Paddington Station. On Monday morning, I asked my workmate to swap shifts with me so that I could get Thursday afternoon off like she did. When Thursday afternoon finally came along, I went to see her in Sutton. We walked through Nonsuch Park and afterwards Rita invited me to *coffee and cake* in a place that I'd normally never dream of setting foot in. However, the English waitress greeted Rita with a certain familiarity, although she also seemed a little surprised. When she took our order and went off to get it, Rita told me that she always spent her free Thursday afternoons in that café, but always went alone.

On Sunday, we met up again in Portobello Road, but we left early and went to have dinner somewhere quieter. The following Sunday, I took Rita to Brighton for the first time. It was June, and although the English summer didn't officially begin for another two weeks, the *outdoor* life already beckoned, and in London and Croydon it seemed as if the bustle became more festive, and work lighter and things didn't matter so much. Many Londoners must have felt the same, because Rita and I caught the train in East Croydon, which had come almost full from Victoria, with you and Jim in some coaches at the rear. That's how the season's first trip to Brighton began.

You seemed surprised to see Rita turn up: I remember that well. You knew each other from Portobello Road, of course, but it's my impression that you never stopped being a vague and uncomfortable presence for each other. You had gone to London when you were twenty; Rita, when she was ten years older. You were not seeking the same thing, you hadn't left behind the same thing. For you, Veiga was always a different time; Rita's time went by in London just as it did in Coruña. When I went out to smoke in the corridor with Jim, I heard you asking each other about work, family, how good or bad life was in Willesden Green or Sutton. When I went back into the compartment, I was amazed at how calculating your friendliness towards each other had become through contact with that country. Jim, who was with me, didn't seem to notice anything. On Brighton beach, while Jim bought ice cream for the four of us and Rita went back to the changing rooms for her straw hat, you asked me:

'So how long have you been with her?'

There was no trace in your voice, in your joking expression, of that so finely calculated courtesy that you had shown towards my new girlfriend on the train.

'It can't have been long,' you ventured when you saw that I took my time in answering. 'A week? Two? And where did you meet her again? She wasn't working with you anymore, was she?'

The English sun, which I hadn't had the chance to see much of that summer in Brighton, pierced my eyes, and that and the clumsy interrogation made me feel uncomfortable. I didn't like to think that you were jealous, or that you were disappointed in not having influenced my decision as much as you would have liked. And I appreciated even less, as your tone of voice suggested, that all that was just a joke to you, just like *gossiping* with your workmates from Marks and Spencer while smoking in the break. Rita was surely not the prettiest or liveliest girl that I could take to Brighton, but as strange as it might seem to you, over those two weeks I had already developed a solid and strange, as well as unexpected, affection for the cook from Sutton. I didn't like to think that all that was for you, who were still my best friend in London, perhaps just a joke.

Then Jim turned up with his giant baby's grin and ice cream cones for everyone, and I couldn't answer. Shortly afterwards, Rita appeared too with her straw hat and cheeks bright red from the heat and the effort of looking for her things in one of those changing rooms that are stuffed with English girls. The conversation gradually went back into English. Jim didn't speak another language and even you and Rita, who had both gone with the English to settle into their domains, had lost the habit of speaking in our language. I was gradually left out. I'm not good at English and never will be. And I regret that I won't be, although at times I would like to be able to plunge into it, lose myself, go unnoticed, like you both learnt to, each in your own way, Rita and you.

From the outside, I watched you speak in English from Willesden, from Harrow (where Jim had been born and grown up, a post-war English boy), from Sutton, from Indians and Pakistanis and the Caribbeans who lived in each of those places, and I thought about how English you might seem if someone could turn the sound off in that scene, if the imperfect accents that you two women had would disappear and Rita were left in a plastic seat, covered by her straw hat and parasol (because she's very pale and you know she gets burnt easily), and you sat with your legs crossed over the towel and Jim lying beside you with a hand distractedly resting on your knee. And that's how it went by: you speaking, me watching you and looking at all those English people in their bathing costumes, and the dark green sea that stretched for miles and miles beyond, to Veiga, that first Sunday of the season on Brighton beach.

For many weeks, the bare hour that went by from when Rita met me in Croydon on Sundays until the two of us caught the train for Brighton, was the only moment when I was alone with her, with the person who was now my girl. The first time that I could really be alone with her, one Thursday when Tino was working and the Italian had gone back to Bari for the holidays, I was surprised at how soft her skin was beneath her clothing, and at how warm her breath was, and how deep her abandon could be, unthinkable in an English cook, unthinkable also in a thirtysomething woman from Coruña, who apart from the extravagant affair with Tino had only had one boyfriend when she was sixteen. The following Sunday, Rita didn't catch the train to Brighton because that same day she left for Cornwall with her bosses, the Raymonds, who didn't want to go without their cook for the obligatory fortnight's holiday on the coast. I missed her and felt a

certain unease, when looking at the calendar, that we
were now in August and fewer and fewer Sundays were
left for us to go to Brighton beach with you and Jim.

Sometimes, you and Rita would lie on your towels
(Rita always with her hat on under the parasol) whilst we
men would strike up a man's conversation. It wasn't easy
because my English was still feeble, and I knew nothing
(and still don't) about British politics, nor did I have a car
or a garden (I don't have a car now; a garden, yes). We
almost always ended up talking about football and Jim
chose to ignore very elegantly my clumsiness with gram-
mar and the subtlest details about English football.
Sometimes I would look at you and see that you were
leaning on your elbow and were listening without hearing
us, whilst at the same time gazing at the horizon or puff-
ing on a cigarette. Of the four of us, you were the least
adult but you tried to compensate for this by becoming
the protectress, the group's mother, a benevolent and
modern mother always worried about her own. You had
begun to let your hair grow and no longer painted your
eyes with a dark line above and below, like Twiggy. I did-
n't know the influence that Jim had had on all that, but
he seemed to observe his new girlfriend's gradual evolu-
tion with pleasure.

It was on the second of the three Sundays when Rita did-
n't visit Brighton that you appeared with a book in English.
You normally brought (I remember it well) some little
romantic novel in Spanish that you had found in the shop
in Ladbroke Grove, where, when we were bitten by home-
sickness, we would buy turnip tops and salt pork, and which
also satisfied those whims you had to read in a language
whose written form you understood. Lying face down on the
towel whilst Jim and I talked about our business, you were
reading and scribbling things for a good while.

'I'm going to learn English,' you simply told me when Jim went off to buy ice cream and we were left alone, like when we really were best friends.

'But you already know English,' I replied. Of all the people I knew from Portobello Road, you were the one who best spoke English. Sometimes even I didn't understand you. That caused some people in Portobello Road to look at you suspiciously, and you know it, as if you wished to cross over to the other side that didn't belong to you, as if English and miniskirts and dyed hair were little stigmas that made you an outsider to your own kind.

'Yes, I know a bit. But to speak with people in the street and with customers and add things up in Marks and Spencer. But I hardly know how to read or write it. And I'd like to.'

You began to talk to me about a *college*; until then, I didn't know that word. A college in West Hampstead close to where Jim had his flat, a college from where he saw Indians and Blacks and Italians emerge each evening, all with books under their arms. It was all decided now: you had gone a few days before to enrol in English and Maths too, and this time you hadn't told me a thing, I couldn't follow your movements closely like Jim could, who I imagined convincing you that you still had time to learn, that your more than average time in the school in Veiga meant nothing in that brand-new country. And hatching other plans with you that I preferred to know nothing about.

'It's three days a week, from seven to ten. I'll have time to have a *sandwich* after work. And on other days, I can study at home.'

'And how are you going to get from Hampstead to Willesden Green at ten at night?' I replied. 'There are hardly any buses after ten'.

You lowered your voice to answer, although on Brighton Beach probably nobody else understood Galician, and if they did, what you were going to say would not make waves like it would have done in Veiga if it had ever occurred to you to say such a thing there.

'Well, on days when I can't get the last bus, I can stay at Jim's house. It's virtually right beside the college.'

I wanted to ask if it had been Jim's idea to learn English, the only language he knew, and to judge by the strange expressions he made when he saw us speak in our own language, the only language he believed existed in the world. But instead I just said:

'And do you need Maths too?'

'Yes, Maths and English this year. Perhaps next year I can take up another subject. And they told me at the college that the following one I could go to university.'

In Veiga, when people your age were becoming grown up, that word now had a meaning, a form; it was no longer a feeble idea full of mystery as it had been for those of my generation and me. But that didn't mean that the road was easy. Out of those who went to school with you, two or three went off to Lugo afterwards to do teacher training. You hadn't been one of them and you never wanted to be, or at least I never noticed. You'd stopped going to school at fourteen, weren't interested much in what they taught you there or the never-ending and somewhat absurd power games with the school mistress and other pupils, and you felt, above all, a certain remorse in making your mother send money every month that could surely have been better spent on something else. For example, opening a haberdashery. Your mother always used to say (I remember her just before she left for Bilbao, when I was just a little boy) that when she had enough saved up, she wanted to return to Veiga and open a haberdashery. And for a few years, between your leaving school and leaving for London, that had been your dream in the Barreses' house. Teresa would send money and granny Amalia kept some back for household expenses, as she had always done, and saved some of it. You had also started to work, first as a domestic in a house in Castropol, and then, when they opened the stationer's shop they took you on as a sales assistant. All your wages went towards the haberdashery. But at some point, when Luísa had suddenly announced her marriage and Lidia's family needed someone to make up the quartet to go on the emigration expedition, you had decided to go to London. Teresa, based on what you had told me, was still a domestic in Bilbao. She was probably on the verge of being able to return to Veiga and open that haberdashery she yearned for, but at that time I didn't know if your project was still on. Once, many years later (remember?), when the two of us were alone in my shoe shop, you told me:

'My mum sees me working in a shop, my granny tidying up and her doing the accounts. It's all she dreams about and hopes from life.'

And many years later, on Brighton beach, in a country where there were no haberdasheries or families of three generations of women who lived in the same house, you told me, just as surely as you had told Jim days and who knows whether weeks before:

'Nurse. I want to be a nurse.'

Of course, when anyone looked at you, they couldn't say that they were seeing the ideal nurse, but I forced myself to congratulate you and say that I was sure that you were going to be a very fine nurse. And I wasn't lying. If you had left Veiga without a mother, without a husband, and had reached London and managed to become more English than I would ever be, with an English boy and English job and at an English school and everything else, you could also become a nurse however much your personality appeared to be at odds with that.

Hampstead

We brought the beach season to a close on the first Sunday in September. The English summer was coming to an end, and when it ends you know it's over; it doesn't have those comebacks in late September that the summer in Veiga had when we were both there. Also, you were starting your classes in the college in West Hampstead the following week and wanted to spend your Sundays studying, like one of those dedicated schoolgirls you never were. Once back, when the train was almost touching the platform at East Croydon, we two couples said our goodbyes with the promise of chatting on the phone regularly, having lunch one Sunday and visiting each other. But the four of us knew (or at least it seemed that way to me) that our unusual association was not going to be able to survive beyond Brighton.

And it didn't. Once that summer shared in Brighton had ended, the four of us were never together again. What did survive was your determination to learn to read and write in English, and it even survived the harshest days of winter, from the first of December onwards, when it gets dark at four in the afternoon and never dawns before eight, and the cold hits your body with a thud as soon as you step out into the street. You kept going to the *college* in West Hampstead three times a week and staying at Jim's house when you didn't have time to catch the last bus, and studying in your room on Sundays. In January, not only did you also sign up for Maths, but they also put you in a more advanced English class because you were making quicker progress than your classmates. When I found all this out through increasingly distant conversations, I felt strangely proud, although I never would have dared tell anyone. I also thought that Jim must have felt even prouder, and that left a certain bitter taste in my mouth.

Now we had so few times to see each other (Sundays in Portobello Road had become a rarity, whether because of Jim's opposition, or the time you had to spend studying), that I even dared to go and see you a few times in Marks and Spencer on Oxford Street, the temple of *Englishness*, your temple too back then. There I discovered that, deep down, you were beginning to give up. The job at Marks and Spencer had been alright at the beginning: after those small efforts at the Waycott Hotel, there was nothing like moving between hangers and mannequins dressed with those clothes that were so correct but with an eccentric touch that English women of a certain age liked so much, and at the same time it had become monotonous. The false smiles, the *What can I do for you?* and the *Thank you, come again*, the women customers who at the beginning were delighted to be attended to by the new and pretty girl but who twisted their noses as soon as you opened your mouth and revealed your accent.

When I surprised you acting, and successfully (or so it seemed to me), in ways that I had only seen before in English women (Mrs Stobart, the two daughters, the women customers in the restaurant, and one of those women who I happened to sit facing on the train or underground), at first, I found it funny; then it became serious. Because if you had become so English to my eyes, to all the Galicians in Portobello Road, you would be a lot more so when surrounded by them, in your section in the basement, *Women*, in the Marks and Spencer on Oxford Street (that was where you started; afterwards, some section manager happened to say that you had something of a French girl about you, and so they put you on *Parfumerie*). And much more with Jim in his bachelor *flat* in West Hampstead, the two of you sharing that improvised privacy you had three nights a week when you finished English classes and it was too late to go on by bus to Willesden Green. Jim was lucky. He had got an exotic girl, a girl who could easily pass for Italian or French and who for that reason surely prompted looks of admiration among his friends down the *pub*, but who seemed at the same time to want to become English and would surely not protest if he suggested buying *Fish and Chips* for supper on a Sunday and going for a walk on Hampstead Heath even when the weather threatened rain. I couldn't imagine the English girl you would be when alone with Jim, with that Jim who I now recall with fear, because perhaps he had something to do with your disappearance. I didn't want to think that with or without classes you'd learnt English so well that you could talk endlessly with Jim like another Elisa had talked to me back in Miou.

City

Elisa-Luísa from Willesden Green. Elisa-Liz from Oxford Street. After what happened in Croydon, you didn't go back to Marks and Spencer. Your bosses agreed with you that to carry on in the shop in Oxford Street, with Jim a step away in the offices, wasn't the best idea, but they regarded you as a good worker and offered to transfer you to one of their branches in the suburbs, or even pull strings so that another shop in Oxford Street could take you on if you preferred to leave. But you didn't want to have anything more to do with shops and you hadn't been at the college in West Hampstead long enough to aspire to secretary or clerical jobs. The end of the relationship with Jim had caused you to settle permanently in the house in Willesden Green, which you had recently abandoned for weeks at a time, but you didn't want to ask Nela to get you back into the Waycott Hotel. I'd heard that Mr Stobart was looking for a pair of new waiters, but I didn't know what Rita would think if you started working with me, so I didn't say anything to you. Finally, the opportunity came along (in our community, the Galicians in London, it always did, even though it might take a miracle) through Dolores and Marta, two spinsters from the bar in Portobello Road who cleaned offices at night in the City. It was tough, it was boring, it was badly paid and you could easily get the feeling, with the mop and dust cloth and the scouring pad in your hand, that a cloak of invisibility had fallen over your shoulders as long as the shift lasted. And then another made of drizzle, cold and light at the wrong time when it finished.

Ten at night *in*, six in the morning *out*. It was the time when the days began to grow shorter and you, who would sleep well into the afternoon, began to spend weeks on end without seeing sunlight. That was what you told me, months later, when all of those who were not going back to spend Christmas at home gathered in Portobello Road on Christmas Eve. You didn't see me during all that time either. You no longer had the impression of living in London, or Veiga, or anywhere in this world. Now you simply lived by night.

At the beginning, you came and went each day to Willesden Green. On the outward journey, you found the underground almost empty, always afraid that some strange type would sit next to you and make you feel embarrassed for no reason: that happened in London, but not in Veiga. On the return journey, you seemed to cross paths with all the rest of London that was going to work when you had already finished. When you entered the house in Willesden Green, Lidia and Nela had been gone for almost two hours, but it coincided with Celestino being unemployed over those weeks, and he couldn't think of anything better to do than moving about the house and not letting you rest. That was why when Dolores and Marta offered you a room that had become vacant in their flat in Bethnal Green, you didn't have to think twice about it. You felt relieved and to some extent happy to be able to leave that house. You had led Lidia to understand that you now no longer wanted more boys, or dances, that the thing with Jim hadn't been an apparently serene interval before returning to the life of an English spinster that both of you enjoyed so much, and Lidia didn't seem to have handled the loss of her fellow adventurer very well. At that time, she was *between boyfriends* and needed someone to go with her to the Soho clubs on Friday and Saturday nights.

I knew that Dolores and Marta were from the Ourense area, and that the former was a widow and the latter had never been married and left behind a child. Since they had arrived in London, years before me, more or less at the same time as Tino (they were amongst the first), they had always worked in office cleaning, always at night, and for them the darkness was now a realm of their own. Perhaps that is why in spite of being both good women and treating you with the kindness reserved for a younger sister, they never showed too much sympathy when you would sleep until just before beginning your shift and didn't do your household chores. Not even when you spent weekends dozing in the kitchen, wrapped in a blanket and with the television on (the only luxury in that modest dwelling), while they went dancing down the Portobello Road.

When I saw you on Christmas Eve, at six or seven in the evening, you still didn't seem as used to the nocturnal life as Dolores and Marta, who at that very moment were beginning to flourish and were dancing on the floor with a pair of waiters from Twickenham. The three of you had worked the night before until six in the morning, as always, and now you had two nights off. Dolores and Marta had slept until two in the afternoon and then started trying on outfits, trying out the hairstyles they saw in magazines, putting on makeup like Jean Shrimpton. They had been waiting for the Christmas Eve party in Portobello Road for weeks. They woke you at five and almost had to force you to get dressed and put on make-up. You didn't know what day it was. You thought that in a few hours you would have to get on the bus again and go to the lawyer's practise in Carey Street, or the skyscraper offices in Cannon Street, any place where you were sent that day by the night cleaning agency that Dolores and Marta had got you working for.

'Are you coming to Croydon tomorrow for Christmas lunch?' I asked as you covered your eyes like a bat, blinded by the lights that came from the dancefloor. The Elisa from Willesden Green would now be in the middle of all that racket, dancing. 'The restaurant is shut, but the Stobarts left the kitchen to Tino, me and some other workers and we're going to make lunch there and then all get together in the dining room. Other people are coming too. Rita's coming to help us with the cooking, and some girls she knows in Sutton.' At that moment you, who with Jim had been so prim, so proper, so English, couldn't avoid showing the disgust in your eyes. I thought then that you wouldn't return to Croydon after that day, after what happened to you in Croydon, and that this was the idea that was making you retreat. But it wasn't that. You were just tired.

'Tomorrow I think I'll stay at home and rest. I already made arrangements for *Boxing Day* with Dolores and Marta. They say they want to go St Albans on the train from King's Cross, to get to know the country a bit better. I can't believe we've been in England so long and we only know London, can you?'

'Well,' I replied. 'You know Brighton too.'

'Yes, I know Brighton too.' That Christmas Eve afternoon, Brighton beach, the timid English sun in July and August didn't seem to be just sixty miles from Notting Hill, but far, far away, much further than Veiga over the sea, a thousand seas between.

So, when the Christmas Eve party in Portobello Road ended, I said goodbye once again for several months. Bethan Green and the City were too far from Portobello Road and from Veiga and Croydon. I spent Christmas Day cooking first and then eating at The Two Roses, and on Boxing Day I went to Sutton on the bus to fetch Rita who was going to spend some days with me until her bosses returned from Scotland, where they had gone to spend New Year's Eve with a married daughter who lived near Glasgow.

Together on the morning of the second day, the twenty-eighth, while I shaved in the bathroom and Rita still dozed in the bedroom (she wasn't sleeping well either because of the night shifts, although not as much as you: every day she had to stay awake until her employers went to bed, in case one of them fancied an *omelette* for *supper*), I realised that I had never spent so much time with someone who by then had been more or less my official girlfriend for more than a year. And it didn't bother me. When I took her to Brighton with you and with Jim and you or when we went to Portobello Road with other people, Rita wasn't brilliant, she wasn't a people person, it wasn't fun being with her. But alone, in that conjugal, improvised intimacy, Rita revealed herself to be surprisingly warm, with an almost unlimited capacity to listen and a natural ability to be quiet when I most appreciated silence. That's why, on the third day, when Rita suggested over lunch and without stating names or faces, that marriage could be a good option for an emigrant couple who were not youngsters any more but still not old and alone in the world, I listened attentively and quietly asked myself why I hadn't thought of that before. On the last night of the year, which we didn't spend in Portobello Road because we were afraid that the trains to Victoria would be too full, but in a Portuguese bar in Croydon, I asked Rita to marry me. It was just before eleven, whilst we were still waiting for Tino, who was going to come along with a new female companion, and another two or three friends of mine. She didn't seem surprised at all; she simply said yes. Afterwards, we hardly had time to talk any more about the wedding, because the others soon arrived and at brief moments throughout the night, amid the noise, I even managed to forget that I would soon be married to Rita.

The wedding was in February, in the Church of Our Lady of Reparation in West Croydon. I had been there several times already, almost always when someone from the Spanish community in Croydon was getting married, baptising a child or died, because that was the parish that those who wanted to or could continue practising their religion after arriving in London made their own. Davide, the Neapolitan who lived with Tino and I, was one of those people, and it was precisely thanks to him that I got the priest of Our Lady of Reparation to publish the *banns* in the church in mid-January and the date was set for the first week in February.

We didn't tell too many people: we weren't young anymore and it wasn't Veiga. Almost nobody there knew our intentions, and over the following months one person after another was successively surprised to find out that we were husband and wife. Rita did let the Raymonds know, and in spite of being so English that they could not conceive of any another civilised form of religion than that of the Church of England, they came to the ceremony at Our Lady of Reparation. In truth, I thought, as the priest read us the vows that sounded so worn out in Castilian and in Veiga, in English and in Croydon they were still adorned with a certain British solemnity. Our situation would be a lot simpler if we accepted Raymond's proposal for Rita to stay on with them in their house while they were prepared to offer me work as a gardener, butler or whatever. All I had to do was hand in my *notice* at The Two Roses, look for someone who could take my room and begin a new life in that part of London called Sutton, far from Portobello Road, Bethnal Green, far from you, a place where you couldn't come to visit me like you had done in Croydon. I never told you until now, but I thought about that as the priest kept reading in a language which I understood increasingly less, whilst Rita and I signed our names in the registry (an unexpected clue to our passage through London), as our friends and acquaintances gathered around the newlyweds to offer their congratulations.

I was still thinking about it on my wedding night. It wasn't by any means the first night that Rita and I had spent together. From the beginning of our relationship, with the trips to Brighton with Jim and you, we both tended to sleep (when we did sleep) in my room. But that pokey place, without enough light and above all with the interminable racket made by Tino and the Italian on the other side of the wall, hardly seemed suitable. Rita and I didn't have a house to play in, like almost all couples have in the world, and like I had the first time I got married. Very early the next morning, we left for the Isle of Wight on honeymoon. That was a luxury, an extravagance, something that we would never do if the Raymonds hadn't given Rita three days off without her asking, as well as a generous present which they suggested, with British subtlety, she should invest with her husband in discovering that part of the country we most wanted to see. Rita and I didn't mind going anywhere. We only knew London and Brighton, but we would never miss the rest of the country; we didn't know what was further to the north, or to the east, and we weren't bothered either. Finally, Mrs Raymond timidly dared to suggest that fifty years beforehand, she and her new husband, who at that time had just returned miraculously intact from the front in France and the Great War, had spent a marvellous week on the Isle of Wight. It seemed like a good idea to me, and that very afternoon I went off to buy two train tickets and passages on the ferry for after the wedding.

For the night before, we had decided to take a room at a hotel near Waterloo, to be able to arrive on time for the first train that left for Portsmouth. The Mad Hatter was the name of that place. It wasn't a luxury hotel, but certainly better than what we could afford: the Raymonds' gift had been very generous. While Rita, sitting on the bed with me lying beside her, slowly removed the black tights that she had premiered that day, I thought that I'd never had so much time to be so alone with her, but I also thought that I wasn't afraid at all. Being with Rita, lovely Rita Meter Maid, in a hotel room to the south of the Thames was not every different to being with Inés in Veiga on our first wedding night, the two of us so innocent; even the darkness of the *borough* of Lambeth wasn't so different to what dominated, fifteen years beforehand and in more ways than one, Veiga. I already knew all that, and at the beginning I didn't think about you: I only thought about Inés and felt a slight tightness in my chest. But afterwards, Rita timidly stretched towards the switch and turned off the light, and that was when I began to miss you, and Inés disappeared, and Rita too, almost, in spite of me being alone with her in that room in a hotel in Lambeth. Because Rita was silent. She didn't say another word all night. Rita was silent. And I felt then, with immense pain, just as I've felt again recently because this time it's true, that in some way your words were now lost to me forever.

The arrival of the really good weather, which in London, after several hesitations, false starts and setbacks, is always delayed until at least May, also brought an unex-

pected turn of good luck for me and Rita. Firstly, one of
the cooks at A Torre, a Portuguese restaurant in Croydon,
died suddenly in the kitchen itself. I heard it in passing
that very afternoon from the assistant in the *off-licence* as
I bought tobacco. Back then, rumours travelled through
Croydon the same way they still do in Veiga; now,
Croydon seems more and more like the City, Soho and
Bayswater, and I hastened to tell him that I had a wife, an
excellent cook who got on with the job and who was
looking for work. The Portuguese were really *pressed for
time*; they interviewed Rita the next day and the day after
that gave her the job. By coincidence, a couple I knew,
from the Viveiro area, had gone back to Galicia and left a
small two-bedroom apartment vacant. I did them a
favour by taking it, because they hadn't given notice on
time and the landlord wanted them to pay several
months up front. And that way, all in a hurry, the same
way that the good weather always comes to London,
Rita's and my true married life began.

Conjugal life also meant a return to certain old habits,
like visiting Portobello Road on Sundays. Rita and I
turned up there on the first Sunday in June. It had been
almost two years since we had begun to go together and
with Jim and you to Brighton, and that, even in summer,
even with the same weather, seemed like another country.
Portobello Road did too. It wasn't that we were hoping to
make a triumphal entry, but once there we realised that
we hardly knew anyone. Many had left, like the couple
from Viveiro who had given us their apartment, and others had arrived. London is like that: an animal that
changes before your very eyes; London isn't like Veiga.
Perhaps that's why I was happier when I saw an out-
stretched arm that greeted me from the tables and when,
squinting, I confirmed it was you.

You got up from your chair, came towards me, gave me a hug, and afterwards kissed me on the cheeks. Your happiness was expansive, fraternal, slightly childlike, like that of a little girl who meets up with cousins she is very fond of after not seeing them for a while. That was also your first evening in Portobello Road in a long time, as you confessed. Your hair was tied up in a ponytail, face washed, you wore jeans and a dark blouse that seemed too large and which Dolores had lent you, according to what you told me later. Now you hardly had any garments that weren't from work. You now seemed used to the night that you had so disliked at the beginning: you were one more of its inhabitants who from time to time paid a visit to the land of daytime. But that had now ended: now you never come and visit in the morning light. You don't come and visit me.

We talked about the wedding, about Rita and my new place in Croydon, and her new job. For a second, it seemed as if was the old times again in Oxford Street, the times when I was your best friend in London and Croydon still hadn't happened. Your life hadn't changed much, you admitted as you lit up one fag after another. You were still employed in the night cleaning agency that sent you to a lawyer's practise one week and to a skyscraper another (but always in the City, that miniature city through which London's blood seemed to throb) and sharing a flat in Bethnal Green with Marta and Dolores.

'They're good girls,' you commented. 'Now I get up at four and five in the afternoon and do what I have to do in the house and they don't moan so much. But sometimes they get on my nerves a bit with their complaints. About the *union*, above all.'

'The union?' I'd heard about the unions, of course, ever since I had got to Croydon, but I'd never belonged to one and I hardly knew anyone who did, or at least not among the community of Italians, Greeks and Spanish in which I lived. The unions, workers' rights, defence against bosses, *welfare* and *civil rights*: those things that we didn't seem to be invited to.

That was around February or March time. You had been working for the cleaning agency for four or five months, but you still couldn't cope with the nightshifts. They had already threatened to sack you once or twice, because between the racket of the house in Bethnal Green and the morning light, sometimes you didn't get to sleep until midday and didn't wake up in time to catch the quarter-past-nine bus in the evening. Or you would turn up in the wrong building and lose time calling your supervisor at home and then looking for transport to get there. That Wednesday (or Thursday, because you had started your work on Wednesday, and but for the tide that silently filled the City streets it was now Thursday) seemed like just another day. You would get on the bus, arrive in Bethan Green, and if lucky quickly fall asleep and wake up at three or four, and if unlucky you'd spend hours tossing and turning in bed. Sometimes you had to work with Dolores or Marta in the same building, or with some other girls from back home, or Andalusians, or Portuguese, or Italians, and those were the good weeks. No, it wasn't bad work either with some of the Irish and English girls. The worse was when they would put you with girls who had just arrived in London from the Caribbean or India and hardly spoke English, or when you had to clean offices that were so small the agency decided that they only needed you and you were alone. Then you could spend entire days without uttering a single word.

That period was one of those. You left the Blackfriars

building in which were crammed the four small offices you had to clean on your own, lit a fag (once they surprised you smoking at work, and they didn't like it), and headed along New Bridge Street in the direction of the bus stop. You had hardly taken a step when two women stopped you.

Short and curly hair, dark skirt and sweater, bags under their eyes like someone who has had a sleepless night. Cleaners too. You even reckoned you had already seen the taller of the two in the agency's offices when you went to get your *wage packet* (always scarce) on the first of the month.

'Excuse me,' said the shortest and plumpest, with an Irish accent. 'Would you like to join a union?'

At the beginning, you didn't know what they were asking (living at night slows down the reflexes), and you shook your head. They're wanting money, you thought, and that was certainly something you didn't have enough of. But the tall one didn't give in and handed you a leaflet. *Transport and General Workers' Union*, it said.

'Shall we go and have a tea and a chat?' the short one suggested.

A tea seemed like a better idea. The cold at six in the morning around Blackfriars, beside the Thames, was always like a punch in the stomach when you went out, even when you'd been cleaning an office building for eight hours with the heating off. And if there was something you had learnt in London, it was that tea could definitely heal the wound left there by the cold, and a lot of other wounds too. I remember quite well that day in Croydon when you came over, and you didn't want a tea. Perhaps that's why things went the way they did.

You went into Blackfriars Station, protected from the cold, and bought three cups of tea there. You were sleepy and confused. When you left work, you always went straight home, and now you didn't know what time you were living or where all those people were coming from who were going through the Tube doors hardly glancing at the three women who were sipping tea, sheltering in a corner.

'We've been chasing after all the night cleaners for nearly two months. We leave at six in the morning to find them when they finish work,' began the short one, who had introduced herself as Mary. 'We thought that we had talked to nearly all of them, but we'd never seen you.'

'It's important that us night cleaners get together,' replied the other, Sheyla. 'That way they won't dare to make us keep changing buildings every week, do cleaning without any heating in winter and, above all, pay us these rotten wages.'

You nodded mechanically at that speech which perhaps Sheyla had down to a tee and well rehearsed, but it didn't have the effect on you that she probably intended. Your wage was not only less than half of what you earned at Marks and Spencer, but was also quite below what you earned at the Waycott Hotel when you first arrived in London. You had hardly noticed it because now your life was reduced to going from work to home and from home to work and your only expenses were the rent and a bit of food, and now there were no more of those Sundays in Portobello Road, drinking one beer after another, Saturday mornings at the flea market in Camden Town and the hairdressers every first of the month, even though it was those cheap African girls who were a bit shambolic.

'That's why we need the union,' Mary went on. She also seemed to bring her well-rehearsed speech from home. 'At the moment we're with the Transport and General Workers' Union, with the T & G. But let's not kid ourselves. We need a union of our own. All the T & G does is look down its nose at us'. Here Mary dropped the pleasantries; her words were more cutting, with that sharp edge that English words sometimes have when they are said in a hurry or with disdain. 'They think that we don't really need to work, that we get all we deserve for daring to leave the house. But they're a union and they can't slam the door in our faces just like that. It's what the law says.'

That was in February or March, and then you hardly knew what a union was (who, born in Veiga around 1945, would know? Of course, I knew a bit more, but not as much as I should have. Dad was a trade unionist: that was all I managed to coax out of my mother, that Dad was a trade unionist). Three months later, you told me that first Sunday in June in Portobello Road, it was you who went out to look for the other early morning cleaners, after work, to talk to them about the union. There were not many left in the City who didn't know about the trade union, but you had decided that there would be no one who didn't know about you. After finishing your ministry, you went off to sleep, and when you woke, had something to eat and left for Mary and Sheyla's house, where you would write pamphlets and make lists of demands and prepared the Saturday meetings with the other cleaners and the Wednesday ones with the people from the T & G. You liked the former. The latter, not so much. As the weeks flew by and disappointments occurred, you ended up having the same opinion about them as Mary and Sheyla.

'I can't hardly sleep on Wednesdays, because the T & G shuts at five and they won't see us after half past three. And there's no way they'll come and see us at the night offices, or on Saturdays, which is the only time when we can all meet. Sooner or later we'll have to say goodbye to them. But for now…'

On the train back to Croydon, I dared to comment to Rita, who was sat right at the back with the other Galicians, that I was happy to see you alive again, and talking almost non-stop, and moving your hands and eyes when you spoke, and Rita replied:

'Yes, that girl always needs something new to get her going. Two years ago, it was that Jim, a year ago it was English classes, now it's this union… I wonder what it'll be next year. I hope it's not my husband.'

And it was then, on the train from Victoria to East Croydon, just before Clapham Junction, when I realised that Rita had known all that time, perhaps she had known the same day you had knocked on the door of my house in Croydon, crying, while she was in Sutton, or perhaps it had been before, or perhaps afterwards, but she had known for some time, and I had a strange feeling, as if Rita had come into my life in Veiga, my life and your life in Veiga, without warning, and I didn't like it because Rita wasn't from Veiga, perhaps she was from Coruña or from London at the same time, but not from Veiga, never from Veiga. The Veiga that had become a strange place, with Rita living there and an Elisa who was breaking away more and more from the Elisa from Veiga. It wasn't that I didn't like the Elisa from London, the one who went to the City at night to clean, who lived in Bethnal Green, who was organising the cleaners into a trade union hardly knowing how to read and write. Only that at times you seemed too much like the city, and I had the impression that I could hardly distinguish you from the merciless landscape surrounding you.

That summer, Rita and I spent a fortnight in Coruña. After the honeymoon on the Isle of Wight, other holidays during the same year seemed like a rare luxury, even for the English. This made me think more than it did her; she almost from the beginning had liked the idea of the journey. The push I needed to make up my mind came one Sunday in Portobello Road, one of those many Sundays when you didn't appear. Sat down with a couple who were friends of ours, we were joking about the cost of the rent and potatoes or those small luxuries from back home that one of us would buy from time to time in the shop in Ladbroke Grove.

'And from now on we'll have to get by without certain things,' said Silvana, caressing her swollen stomach. Silvana and Toño had got married over five years ago, just before coming to London, but the first pregnancy had come along when they had already given up all hope. The London air, she tended to joke, was not good for children. 'You'll see what I mean when it happens to you too, you'll see!'

Rita looked serious.

'No. We won't.'

And knowing the children that she'd never had would probably not come along (because my wife didn't want them, or couldn't have them: I never knew which, I still don't know today, and I don't think I ever asked Rita) caused me, from that day, and perhaps unconsciously, to think less about the money I spent, the tobacco and beers for the afternoons lazing in the parks or with friends, and the evenings at the cinema, and all those things that make life in London so attractive. Not that I let myself go completely, because the restaurant plan with Tino was still on, but at least I knew that we could go to Coruña that summer without the world coming to an end. For Tino, however, it did seem to end, because as soon as he found out about Rita's plans, he said, exasperated:

'And do you have to leave right now? Just yesterday I

heard about a Pakistani in South Croydon who wants to sell his off-licence. There, right next to Haling Park, would be ideal for a great little restaurant. I mean, this could be our chance. Perhaps before the end of the year we can say *bye bye* to Mr Stobart.'

But it wasn't the first time that Tino thought he'd found the opportunity of a lifetime for everything then to just vanish without a trace. Once they even ripped him off: he had paid a deposit to reserve some premises, and then his contact disappeared without a trace. Deep down, I thought, Tino hadn't changed much since he'd left Veiga. And in Veiga he was... How do the English say? A *big fish*, a big fish in a little pond, a brightly-coloured and cocky fish with broad fins sweeping everything else aside. But London is a big pond, and here there are a lot of big fish just as striking as Tino, and a lot of them (even if he hates me saying so) are much sharper.

In the end, I asked Tino to go and see the premises whilst we were in Coruña; we would talk when we got back. I didn't believe my friend's caper would come to much, and I wasn't wrong. When I saw Tino again and asked him, he only mentioned problems: too small, the street was too narrow, the Pakistani didn't make a good impression on him. Tino was the same as ever. However, I felt a strange sense of pleasure, and also a certain trepidation to discover that you were not. One Sunday in Portobello Road, as you rolled up a cigarette (perhaps in your meetings with the trade unionists you had taken a liking to roll ups: one of the few good things, you said bitterly, that you had learnt from them), you told me that the cleaners' union was stronger than ever and the strike was imminent.

'At the end of the summer, when they come back, we have to act quickly. Mary, Sheyla and me are trying to get all those who signed up to the union together in the winter, and those who didn't too, to see if we can persuade them. But it's not easy at all. *Fucking bastards*.'

I remained silent before that final outburst of yours. In Portobello Road, we always joked with each other about how easy it was for all of us to end up using *four-letter-words*, but *bastards* was different. You had just worked July and August, but officially you only had a week's holiday. Then the agency let you go with the promise of taking you on again in September. It wasn't that they used the summer to get rid of you that rankled: they did that with everyone, and according to Dolores and Marta, that was what they had been doing for a few years, before they had even arrived in London.

'Bastards,' you repeated again. 'We'll see what they say when I don't clean their offices for a week, a fortnight, a month.'

But I saw a major flaw in your plans.

'But the lawyers and accounts and all those people whose offices you stop cleaning, how is it their fault? Wouldn't it be best to sort it out with the agency?'

You looked at me as I were a small child who still stumbles and hesitates with the language and ways and tricks of grown ups.

'That's the only language they understand,' you simply said.

Then you asked how many hours I worked at The Two Roses every week, and how long my shifts lasted, and how many breaks I had. I felt uncomfortable. I didn't know if it was because of that Elisa, the Elisa who would talk about trade unionism and capitalism, was of course very different to the Elisa from Veiga, the same as Elisa-Luísa from the early times in London, and Elisa-Liz, Jim's girlfriend and employee of Marks and Spencer. But perhaps I didn't like that Elisa so much, or I always thought that the Stobarts treated me well and didn't see the point of so much revolution, above all in a house where you and I were guests. That day you said goodbye for a long time.

'I don't know when I'll be back here,' you said, as if it were an apology. 'Mary and Sheyla told me that in September we're going to have meetings every day to try and call a strike half way through the month. Oh, and I forgot about the college. There is a college up in Bethnal Green. I went to see them and they told me that I could study English again and Maths and Biology too, if I wanted. They agree with me that with not going to classes, I've missed this term, but they think that I can make it up in one year and then send *applications* to a university.'

'Are you still thinking about studying Nursing?' I asked.

You made an ambiguous gesture.

'I don't know. At the start, it was what I most liked the look of, but now I have my doubts. Mary and Sheyla told me about social workers. I didn't know that such a thing existed. They work a lot with social workers in their neighbourhood and Mary even started to study for it, although with her work and family, she never finished. I liked it. As soon as they'd finished telling me all about it, I thought that it's what I'd like to do. Do here in London, I mean. But we'll see. It's going to be a difficult year, with the strike and classes and everything else.'

And then I thought, when wasn't it in London? What year isn't a difficult one in London? Some, because of the cold; others, work; and others, the lack of it. There can't be easy years in London like there were in Veiga. But I didn't say a thing, and kissed you on the cheek and wished you luck at the door of the bar in Portobello Road, in the first chill of September, before you disappeared again, as you tended to do every so often, as you did that last time, into the depths of London, never to emerge again.

Bethnal Green

Sometimes I'm a bit like Tino, and I want to be smart and arrogant and look down my nose at London as if it belonged to me. But then London and you people from London put me in my place. At the start, and for months, I thought that the union was just a union. A trade union. Dad was a trade unionist, which is why he was put in jail. It wasn't my mum who told me that: they told me at my cousin Román's house when I was a young boy. I didn't know what they did in a union. In Veiga, nobody knew, but whatever it was, it couldn't be this. It couldn't be.

Once, in Veiga, when you were little, you were playing with the other little girls and suddenly Valentina turned up and announced that nobody was allowed to play with you, and the others, as obedient as sheep, left you all alone. Not just that afternoon, but all week, all term, all through your school years. You told me that in Veiga many years before, and it was the first thing I thought of when one Sunday I saw Valentina in the bar in Portobello Road, and recognised her (and I could hardly recognise anyone of your age from Veiga anymore, but Valentina I could, and who wouldn't?) and I approached both of you, and you both looked at me for a second, confused, before you announced, in a falsely confident voice and tad louder than was recommendable, as if everyone there had to know:

'Look, Gelo, this is Valentina. She's spending a few days here on holiday with me.'

Valentina's father had arrived in Veiga in '39, as a school teacher. I remembered him when he was young: clean shaven, cocky, very handsome, the father or the older brother that many boys at school wanted to have. Me too, sometimes. His passage through Veiga was meant to be brief, but shortly afterwards he met the person who would become Valentina's mother and requested a permanent post in the town. Twenty years later, he was still the Falange man in Veiga and the proud and handsome (and now slightly grey) father that many children wished they'd had, but who only Valentina had, little Valentina, who could tell the other girls not to play with you and make sure they obeyed her. She had been thin, pale and sickly from birth and hardly went to school (they said that her father taught her at home), but when she was fourteen, her body rebelled and grew and doubled in size. In Veiga, everyone said that she was the same as Ava Gardner, and Valentina perhaps sought to encourage this similarity by combing her hair and dressing and walking like the actress. This didn't stop her being the favourite amongst Miss Brígida's favourites and leading the traditional song and dance group and also the Falangist Youth parade every Victory Day. In Veiga they said that Miss Brígida was already preparing the way for her when she retired.

Valentina on holiday? On holiday at your house? I didn't think I'd be wrong in hazarding a guess that the only holidays that Valentina had known until that moment had been the Falangist Youth camps, and those were far away, very far away from London. Segura wasn't the kind of father to let his daughters go off abroad for a week on their own, much less to Bethnal Green, nor were you someone who would happily open your doors to someone who was living a kind of life you couldn't even dream about. After that first Sunday, I saw you again with Valentina the following one. And after that, according to what you told me, she left, her ten days of rest over before shutting herself away to prepare for a teaching job exam. I didn't tell you then, I didn't feel I had the right to, but I felt a certain nausea at seeing you help build, from your island in Bethnal Green, a Veiga that would never want you, never accept you: the Veiga of Valentina and her father.

I ended up thinking that Valentina's Veiga, the Veiga in which her father could prosper and become a gentleman, was lost, that she wasn't anything other than a cleaner in London, a waitress, a cook who you now helped to take the first steps in a strange country whilst you enjoyed a front-row seat at her downfall. But in London, Valentina, who in Veiga was admired from afar like a second Ava Gardner, was no more than a fairly beautiful face, with perhaps an interesting or moving personal history, but who didn't matter to anyone really, and I didn't think about her again until a month later. It was a Saturday when Rita and I had gone to the dance to meet a group of Portuguese and Italians at a hall belonging to Our Lady of Reparation, the church where we got married. The men talked in our circle about men's things; the women, in another circle, about women's. We always tried to mix, we always tried to remain in the one circle in which those gatherings (although the event was advertised as a dance, not many people did dance, really) began, because even though none of us had observed many English people in similar situations, we thought that the English were like that, they mixed and spoke with each other and that amongst them there wasn't men's business and women's business. The thing is that we always ended up speaking to the same people, like in Veiga or Vilanova or in Caselle Torinese.

But that Saturday, perhaps because we were not in any of those places, but in Croydon, I ended up hearing something that was not meant for me, that was not meant for men. Something about Caterina, an Italian girl who Rita and I had met from the dance at Our Lady of Reparation and who was sort of related to Davide, the Neapolitan.

'And how come Caterina's not here?"

'Ahh, haven't you heard? You won't see her around here, or at the restaurant, or at the church. Disappeared.'

'Has something happened to her?'

'Noooo. She's cooped up at home. Alessandro cleared off, didn't you know? And he left her a little present. That's why she's staying in until she sorts everything out.'

I overheard all that in the women's conversations. I liked Caterina. From time to time, she would come around to see Davide and I always enjoyed having a chat with her: me, in Galician, and she, in Neapolitan. That's why, when later that night Rita and I got home, I asked her what was going to happen with Caterina.

Rita laughed at my tone of concern.

'Don't worry. Alessandro isn't coming back, that's for sure. And Caterina… that's no mystery. She'll put some money together and when she can, she'll go where they can sort the problem out. And then she'll spend a few months staying away from Church, but then she'll be back. Things are different here.'

'What problem?' I was getting more and more confused.

Rita laughed again, showing her tiny, uneven teeth. She even seemed to be enjoying the situation.

'You haven't got a clue, right? You men haven't got a clue.'

Perhaps it was all that game of silences and half-words and connivances that were going over my head, as if I were a small and not very bright child, once more that fatherless child from Veiga, which put into my mouth the reply that I gave you the following Sunday in the bar in Portobello Road, when I had by then managed to fit together all the pieces that you and Rita had ironically thrown at me, whilst you talked of pamphlets and unions and the number of members and demonstrations in front of the Houses of Parliament in Westminster.

'And taking girls away God knows where to sort out these problems is also part of the union's strategy in its fight against capitalism?'

'I did a friend a favour. That's all.' Your answer was swift, almost instantaneous, as if you had already had prepared it, and your voice never sounded nor would ever sound so icy, so metallic, and with that voice you were building a wall for Valentina, as if you wanted to protect her from me, and at that moment I felt immensely sad that you might think that I was the kind of person someone had to be protected from.

'But Elisa! A friend! A friend who in Veiga looked down at you because she was the teacher's daughter and you were the daughter of a single mother, and who will keep doing the same even if one day you decide to go back there. And there's no way she knows what a union is, and if she found out, it would make her laugh.

'We are a women's union. We are sisters. *Sisters*. Everything that happens to a sister is our business,' you simply replied, and cleared off to the bar.

That was something new in your talk, which was increasingly less yours, less of the Elisa that I had known in Veiga, and which became filled with words from newspapers, English words that you used in their original form and adapted without much success to our language. The unity of male and female workers and the struggle against the bosses and the oppression of capital, the emancipation of women and with them of peoples: that was the way you had been talking for almost a year. Perhaps my father spoke like that when he was young, I don't know: if he did, it wasn't with me. But you had never talked of women, or of being a sister to all women. And to be honest, I didn't understand that very well. I couldn't understand it after seeing how different you and Rita were, for example.

I understood it better a few weeks later, one Sunday when you weren't around Portobello Road and I asked Dolores about you. When I saw you there, when you were able to come along, even in the middle of so much racket, conversations, meetings, classes, exams and strikes, you seemed to bloom. Rita always told me, after we said goodbye to you, that it wasn't such a big deal, that you had lost a great deal since you had been working at Marks and Spencer (almost three years ago) and that, in any case, so much activity couldn't hide anything good. According to Rita, you were still in love with Jim and resented not marrying him, leaving Marks and Spencer and inaugurating your glorious life as an English housewife, and deep down the union and the college and everything else were no more than a laugh to try to forget that Englishman. I don't know. Sometimes I am annoyed by the possibility that Rita, who never knew you all those years ago, who never really spoke to you beyond conversations over coffee and cake in Brighton, knew more about you than I did.

'How's Elisa?'

Dolores didn't seem very happy to be asked that question.

'Elisa is looking for a room. On Wednesday, Marta and I sat down with her and told her that she should either change jobs, or leave. At the start, it might not have happened, because we knew that she wasn't well, that it wouldn't be easy for her to leave Willesden and Marks and Spencer and all that, and it didn't bother us so much that at times she might leave the flat untidy or the crockery on the sink. But now she's alright. If she wants to waste her time with the union and the other stuff, good for her, as long as she doesn't bother us.'

You had tried hard to draw Marta and Dolores towards the union. For you, it was a matter of leaving the house tidy, in the metaphorical rather than literal sense, before heading out into the streets in search of unknown sisters. But neither of them had ever seemed interested. Marta was nicer, and had attended a couple of the cleaners' union meetings, more to keep in with you than anything else, but as quickly as it got a little more serious, she soon said that there was no way they would they see her demonstrating in front of the Houses of Parliament in Westminster, that she had gone to London to work, that she would happily accept an increase of two pounds a week (and who wouldn't?), but that she wasn't prepared to go through any bother for that. Several months had gone by since then, but not having attracted your own flatmates to your cause continued to be a thorn in your side. And something similar was going on with me, who you were always telling to join the catering workers' union.

'But there's no such union,' I replied. 'At least, not as far as I know.'

'Then start one,' you replied, implacable as ever. 'Tino and you and two or three more from the restaurant, and then you go around the restaurants in the street. It couldn't be easier.'

But I didn't have any reason to complain at The Two Roses and I couldn't see the sense in starting a union. Dad was a trade unionist. He wouldn't be proud of me. But Dad was from Veiga, and besides, he was dead. You were from London, and you were alive and, as Dolores would say, you lived to waste time on the union. Although now there was perhaps something more than the union.

'And what's the *other stuff?*' I asked Dolores.

It turns out that on her pilgrimage in search of allies to fight against the night cleaning agency, the trade union of Mary, Sheyla and you had ended up distancing itself from the T & G. It sounded a familiar story to me: in recent months, your complaints about the nine-to-five trade unionists had become a real deluge, but I didn't know if the final break had taken place. Dolores didn't know for sure either; she did know that you and your two friends had talked and met with a load of people, whether in a group or not, some looking more hostile than others. And she didn't know that at second hand, but first, because Mary and Sheyla and you lived so precariously that you had to hold some of your trade union meetings in the kitchen at the house on Roman Road. Some of those dodgy-looking types, Dolores assured us, were from the Socialists. And she would say it with the look of fright of someone who had only overheard horror stories about Socialists when she was a very, very small child.

'The International Socialists?' I asked. It's not that I knew too much about that party or others that, most likely, I could never vote for (and I wouldn't mind either), but once Ted (who was an old English divorced guy who had got married to a woman I knew from the Portobello Road and had become widowed in London) told me that he was a member of the Socialists when he was younger.

'I don't know. They said they were Socialists. The thing is that over time the beards stopped coming and the women started. They were Socialists too, or that's what they said. Suddenly, the look on the faces of Mary and

Sheyla and Elisa changed. They said that it was alright
that way, that with women it was alright. And they didn't
bring the Socialists again after that – the women would
sort out everything. Amongst them was Gail. One of
those English girls who are forty and over, fat, her head
unkempt with lots of grey hairs, you know? English
women are not very good at taking care of themselves,
but when they let themselves go like that one... Well,
after that, Gail started to come more and more to the
house. Often it was nothing to do with the union. On the
other hand, Elisa came by less and less and it's not as if
she came much before that, you know. Then Marta and I
knew that they were meddling around the neighbourhood. *Women's liberation*, you'll say. Women's liberation.
That's what they told us.'

Women's liberation, socialism, unionism. The words were
certainly well known; they were words that floated
around the air in England, although at times it was difficult to understand them, just as it is difficult to get the
exact meaning of *righteous* or *cosy* or *conviviality*, because
they have no body, no form, they can't be touched: they
would dissolve immediately in the Veiga air.

'They told us that they were setting up workshops in
the neighbourhood, with the Indian and Arab and Greek
girls and all those people. And they needed those little
pills, you know? Not as if I didn't approve; if I end up with
a bloke here too I'd take them, but man, that's one thing
and another very different is making them available to
everyone. When Marta and I found out, we told them
straight. Marta was even worse than I was, as she doesn't
like those little pills one bit. We told her that if she wanted to keep meddling with Gail then she could find somewhere else to do it. We were fed up with the flat always
being untidy and the lounge busy or full of papers and for-

gotten coats. Not to mention the business of the meetings in the neighbourhood. I don't want some Arab or Indian or Greek coming along, you know what they're like, having a go at me for talking to the wife about the little pills. I don't talk to them, of course not, but those people get the wrong idea about everything and they must think that because we live with Elisa, we're both like her.'

In the end, you found a place to live (right in Bethnal Green, a little towards the south), a room that had become free in Sheyla's building, with a shared bathroom in the corridor, but that didn't mean you immediately started to visit Portobello Road again. Later, I found out that you had argued with Antonio, who was in charge, when you wanted to organise at the premises a talk that you and Gail used to give around Bethnal Green. Antonio didn't want to know anything about the matter and you, who until then always got on well with him, had accused him of being a *pawn of patriarchy*, as you told him in English (everyone who frequented the bar in Portobello Road still remembers it) and of not being bothered at all about women's suffering. Antonio really liked to give off the image of a saintly person, but the years in London had inevitably and gradually softened him up, and even though he would cause a scene every time he would find the lads smoking *joints* in the bathroom, in the end he just let them do it and once even ended up having a few puffs with them; he wasn't an enemy you couldn't win over and get on your side, but on that occasion Lidia stuck her nose in. She said, without anybody asking her for her opinion, that in the end those pills had been going around for years, and she had taken them herself and could even say for sure that all the girls from the bar in Portobello Road who were going with the English lads were taking them, and, if not, anyone who wanted to take them knew how to get them and all without needing to make announcements or organise talks or, above all, get the Women's Liberation out. She said it with contempt, almost spitting it out: Women's Liberation. Just as she said to me whilst she was telling me about it, one afternoon when we bumped into each other in a shop in Ladbroke Grove. For months, I now realise, I only knew about you through what other people told me, and they weren't exactly your best friends.

'Now she's going around with those pills as if they were the great discovery of this Women's Liberation business. Look, nobody can stand her. When she comes to the house for a coffee (my mum invites her round every other Friday), it's all she talks about. The union and the *estraiques*,' Lidia would say it like that, *estraiques* 'and about the Socialists and Women's Liberation and Gail. She doesn't stop going on at me and my mum to join a union. She can't put us in hers, because it's just for night and office cleaners, but she didn't stop until she left us the telephone number and the address of a friend of hers who happens to clean in a hotel.'

I looked at Lidia, who was gesticulating around me, wrapped up in her little white false leather coat and tight trousers with their eccentric pattern (*psychedelic*, as she put it), the two of us walking through Ladbroke Grove towards the Tube station. With long symmetric hair and fringe, and make up that had frozen her permanently at eighteen, she seemed to have travelled a long way since she had left Veiga. I remembered her (of the little I did remember) as a skinny girl, pallid and always sickly. They were from Piantón; her mother used to sell eggs around the houses and she went with her from time to time. She had gone to school when told; she stopped going, too, when told, and there was no girl more devoted than her when she took communion on Sundays, covered by a white veil, no Falangist Youth member more fervent than when she performed in one go and without a single mistake the respective gymnastics routine at the annual exhibition of the Women's Section. It was difficult to see that submissive girl in the Londoner Lidia who would clean through the week from six to two and then chase after the latest lines to arrive at Portobello and Camden markets. Those five years had given her time to learn the names of all the stallholders, one by one, and to know who it was worth haggling with or not. On Friday and Saturday nights, she would dance until she dropped, and every three months she would appear with a new companion which her parents accepted without too much protest, perhaps aware that that was London and London wasn't Veiga, and Lidia, in one place and the other, had only let herself follow the road that others made for people like her, for a poor thirteen-year-old girl in Veiga, for a slightly less impoverished nineteen-year-old girl in London.

'I've already told her: if she keeps on like that, filling people's heads with nonsense when all they want to do is work and earn an honest crust without causing any problems, she'll end up like don Adolfo. Everyone's going to keep clear of her, you wait and see.'

I couldn't help laughing at the comparison. Anyone who had visited the bar in Portobello Road at some point knew who Adolfo was. Anyone who had done so with some regularity also knew that the best thing to do was clear off as soon as they caught a glimpse of the little old man's faded beret, that oak stick that shook in his trembling hands. Adolfo had disappeared from the bar in Portobello Road for months or even years, and you know how the rumours soon start, and some say he died quietly

in his house in Pimlico, and others that got really angry
and will never go back, and some even dare to say that he
went back to Pontevedra now that it no longer seems
such a dangerous business, just as Adolfo himself stopped
being dangerous over the years. But in the end, he always
returns on the arm of his English daughter-in-law; you
and I saw him return two or three times. It's been some
time since the son, some of the most veteran say, could no
longer put up with his father's nonsense. He's been in
London thirty years, half a lifetime, and when more people from Galicia began to turn up in London and Antonio
opened the bar in Portobello Road, he thought that that
was going to be a blessing for his final years. It didn't take
long for him to be disappointed. We only know about one
nation and its imperial glories – they taught us about
them at school and many still love them, and words like
federalism or statute mean nothing. And what's worse,
when Adolfo bothers to explain it to us with infinite
patience, we keep quiet, as if we didn't understand a
thing, as if he were one of those little old English men, as
kind as they are unwelcome, who sit down next to you in
a park and begin to show you photographs of the Great
War that they keep in their wallet. In Croydon, there are
two or three known by the whole and I can't help thinking about Adolfo every time I pass one by. Recently, I
even started to think that you ended up like them too,
that you'll be in some park, on some path in London,
stopping the passers-by, showing them photos and cut-
tings that nobody is interested in.

When I arrived in London, I approached Adolfo somewhat enthusiastically, enthusiastically and in an almost
instinctive way, like a son approaching a father. You don't
know that; hardly anyone knows that, because you
already know what everybody thinks about Adolfo, and

anyone who approached him willingly would soon be entitled to the same opinions. But I immediately had to recognise that the old guy's talk (repetitive and circular, as if, by using the same words so often, the same ideas on his own or with people who didn't understand a thing after a while, his talk went on so long that it became a caricature of what decades before more dignified, wiser men had said) became difficult for me to follow, and even boring. Even so, I'm one of the few people who pay for Adolfo's wine when I see him in Portobello Road, and when I do, I even spend a while listening politely to what he has to tell me. But that's not what I want, of course, for you.

'And did you call in the end?' I asked.

Lidia made an impolite gesture with her hand.

'Of course not! Look, us lot at the hotel are OK. Sometimes it gets tough of course, but that's why we came to London, didn't we? We don't need any union. My mum used to say that I should call the woman Elisa told us about, but then I put that idea out of her head. The truth is that if it weren't for my mum, Elisa wouldn't be coming around our house any longer. But the old girl took a liking to her. I think she's still a little hurt that my sister isn't here, and since Elisa came with us, everything revolves around her, above all now that she's getting on a bit.'

I had already noticed in Portobello Road the particular closeness you appeared to develop with Nela since who knows when; it was, I thought, after the split with Jim and the move to Willesden and Bethnal Green. Since I had stopped being your friend in London, since you had little by little surrounded yourself with women, sisters as you would say. Since then, it was more and more common to see you talking with Nela at a separate table, shielded from the noise of the dancefloor, and you were virtually always holding the hand of the other woman or had placed your hand on her shoulder, because it was no secret that Nela was going blind, and for all I know may be already (in Piantón she had worked a lot sewing trousers and mending skirts and the effect of all those years was showing in her sight), and now, when she speaks with somebody, she needs to feel their hands, fingers, skin. Many young people in Portobello Road think that you are mother and daughter, and are surprised to discover, weeks later, the truth. And then, when Gail appeared, you began to have two mothers in Portobello Road.

Over the years, it became more and more common to see new people in Portobello Road, boys and girls who sometimes, eventually, became husbands and wives, friends, occasional acquaintances. A lot of Portuguese and Italians above all, some English, and in some exotic cases even Indians or Caribbeans. But Gail couldn't avoid attracting strange or even ironic glances as she went by the first time she appeared on your arm on Portobello Road. Over time, the people got used to her as there were times when she would visit the place every week, although those who were young when they turned up there tended to look at her in surprise and then take a look around them, as if to assure themselves that they had arrived where they had intended and not some social club inhabited by eccentric English middle-aged women with greyish long hair and an abundant bosom bulging beneath their black sweater.

Quirky Gail could also have passed for your mother, but that did not seem to make your pretend mother feel jealous. It was not unusual to see the three of you talking with your heads together, like widows at a dance in Veiga, and at times I wondered what you would be speaking about, and in what language. Nela, after so many years, hardly spoke English (communication with the outside world was entrusted to her husband, daughter and even you, and I highly doubted that Gail, like all English people, spoke anything other than her own language), and Gail's talk (for me, an almost impenetrable mass of the words *patriarchy, power structure, sisterhood*) must have seemed as strange as a poem in Chinese to her. Once, as we returned to Croydon by train, Rita suggested that between Gail and you there might be a relationship that was not that of mother and daughter. I looked at her surprised and quite shocked, too. What did I know about those things in Veiga? What could Rita know in Coruña? Rita, quiet and timid Rita, lovely Rita Meter Maid, seemed to know more than I did about stories that bubbled beneath London's surface.

'Besides, you can tell she's a lady,' pointed out Rita without waiting for me to reply. 'For her, this socialism and Women's Liberation business are all entertaining nonsense.' You and Gail, according to what you told everyone, had met each other through the women's section of the International Socialists, in which Gail had been a member temporarily until leaving it quite disenchanted, 'But she can return to her lady's life whenever she wants and Elisa has nowhere to go. She's going to end up the same as with Jim. They're from here; they can entertain themselves with us all they want, but they always have somewhere to go back to. We don't.'

I kept quiet. Rita knew the English better than anyone else from back home, and better than you do, I think; she had lived with an English couple for years, had cooked for them, had all the time in the world (the life of a cook for an old and frugal English couple is not especially demanding) to observe them at her leisure in their own territory.

She knew the English, or rather that particular class of English (I didn't know how to classify them, because they were rich, of course, but very different to the well-known rich people of Veiga, and also those new rich who appeared after the war and who, rather than being wealthy, wanted everyone else at their feet) so well that she couldn't make a mistake in classifying Gail, unkempt and loud Gail, as a product of that particular class. Some months later, I had to finally accept that Rita was right. According to what I knew from what you told me, full of admiration, Gail had indeed studied English at a prestigious university for women on the outskirts of London and had taught intermittently (when she wasn't employed at a school, she dedicated herself to travel) until she had retrained as a social worker, driven by certain vague desires of sisterhood that she had acquired in university and which she had polished until becoming one of the leading figures of the Women's Liberation movement in London. Like that outbreak that at that time the city could no longer ignore, she had behind her a history of temporary alliances, disputes and reinventions that even you found difficult to recall and describe.

For example, her journey through the women's section of the International Socialists had been extremely brief and circumstantial. She had come to the party from a different place than you and your friends, but with the same purpose: to seek allies, no matter how temporary they might be. One after another of you left with your fingers burnt, but the party had at least served for you to meet each other. It had also been some time since Gail had given up social work on the ground in the poorest *boroughs* of London. Now her fight, she said, was beyond the enemy's power structures. The International Socialists, by the way, was also an enemy power structure, and you had understood that very well, assured Gail very seriously, full of reverential respect, and you had expressed it very well, although with other words, in the last and very tense meeting between the night cleaners' union with the party, when you stood up at the table and, shouting in your more broken and ungrammatical than ever English, had accused them of not taking you seriously because you were women and of secretly thinking that twelve and a half pounds per week was enough for you women and of having you making tea and getting the biscuits out before each meeting (with a lot of joking around, of course), but it was always the women who made the tea, because deep down there was no difference at all between their peers and the capitalist exploiters. After that, Sheyla and Mary, who had gone with you to that meeting, and Gail, who was there in her capacity as Female Party Members' Section Representative, also got up, never to return. Now you get by as you can, alone but proud. Or not so alone, because in the fight you had many of London's women's associations behind you, and as for the patriarchy (as Gail maintained, seriously), that did not count.

Now Gail spent her days editing extravagant fanzines and pamphlets, organising talks for women in the poor boroughs to which she had access thanks to her previous job, planning demonstrations and *actions*, and lending a hand in the union. But she thought that someone was still needed to get heavily involved in them, to cast the net (with difficulty and precariously, of course) further to those women who had never suspected that there was more to life than that. She believed that you, with your age, background (nobody was going to suspect someone foreign) and energy could carry out that role perfectly, at least for the time being.

And so, in the autumn, you joined the University's

School of Social Work with Gail's blessing.

'Don't think that I'm doing it for her,' you told me in the bar in Portobello Road, one Sunday when Gail wasn't around. It wasn't as if I had asked you anything. 'You know that I've wanted to become a social worker for ages. But then I met Gail, and it turned out she had done that job, and she encouraged me.'

The School was tough; you had always passed the English courses first in the college in West Hampstead and then in Bethnal Green without any problem, but there you discovered to your surprise and with certain desperation that your more intuitive than precise English was still insufficient for university. The classes and, above all, study at home took up too much of your time and you had begun just to work part time. It had not been easy for you to announce this to your loyalest friends in the union, Mary and Sheyla, because you were afraid that they might regard you as a renegade. Of course, as soon as you obtained the qualification of social worker, you didn't expect to keep cleaning, and that meant that you wouldn't stay in the union either. But they were fascinated by your initiative.

'Brilliant, girl!', Mary had replied. You had told me about it the following Sunday in Portobello Road, blushing with pride, because Mary had been the first to reveal to you the secret network of the night cleaners. That dawn, you and Mary and Sheyla had met for the first time and would go on to become friends, but Mary had been the first to speak. 'I knew that you weren't going to keep cleaning. And it's going to be handy having someone we know in Social Services. You already know how a lot of our colleagues live. We have to get someone into the system.'

You were proud of Mary's words, and rightly so. They

had always called you Elisa; once again, Elisa. Not Luísa, nor Liz. The Liz from Oxford Street, the one who was going out with James Lawford, Harrow born and bred, who sold skirts and perfumes in Marks and Spencer in the centre of London, who liked to go to Brighton in the summer. That Liz was alive just three years before. In the days of Bethnal Green, nobody knew where she was. Today, nobody knows where Elisa from Bethnal Green is.

Croydon

That day it rained hard. It's strange to see it rain heavily here; in London, it always drizzles, all day, without stopping, but it's as if the sky decides never to rain properly, so polite like all the English. There were knocks on the door. I was sleeping in my room and the knocks sounded unreal. Then Davide appeared and told me in that half language of his, the result of the not very successful attempts by Tino me to teach him: you've got a visitor. I thought that he was mistaken. Only Rita visited me, and only on Thursdays and Sundays; even if the Raymonds had given her a day off work on another day, neither she nor I appreciated surprises. But I got up and went to look, and it was you who I found sat on the couch with which we had managed to give the *living room* a certain gentle touch. Your hair was soaked, dark now from so much rain. Your skin and eyes too. Dark, dark.

Davide had remained in the doorway, discreet but with his ears well pricked up. We couldn't stay there. London, for many people, is still their village; in London, everything ends up being found out. Just like anywhere else. We went to my room, and I didn't even try to be *polite* with Davide. In my room, you started to speak to me. It had been some time since you had spoken to me that way, and for that long. But this time it was different. This time it was about Jim. I didn't mind. I just wanted to hear you talk, talk like before, without a single word of that language that not so long before had been unknown to you: the Elisa that didn't know London, Elisa of the Barreses. For a moment, it seemed as if it were you. And I wanted to make sure that it really was you, that it was your hair –

still wet and dark – and your lips, your skin, then your breasts. And, with the curtains drawn, in the half-darkness, I was happy to recover your breath, always so deep, always so calm even in the fiercest of moments, and I confess that on spotting a violet strip that crossed your left wrist I diverted my gaze, closed the curtains and my eyes even more, because I didn't want to see it. I didn't want to see anything that wasn't Elisa from Veiga, Elisa from Miou.

I never knew if you realised that, because when you rolled over beside me with the last moan, you were no longer speaking. You didn't say a single word as you picked up your clothes, scattered across the room, as you quickly got dressed, putting your skirt on backwards, as you fixed your hair at the same time as you were putting your shoes on, as you were going out through the door and crossing the lounge before Davide's somewhere between curious and astonished gaze. You didn't speak. And, in many ways, I think that from that day, you never spoke to me again.

That was when I knew that my Elisa no longer existed.

Miou

London is a city difficult to explain to those who don't know it. Sprawling aimlessly to the north and south of the river, and growing unchecked at all extremes, not even those who were born here always know where it begins and ends. The Stobarts say that Croydon isn't London. But Tino recruited me straight away to come to London, and here I am in London, although here they call it Croydon. London is the only place I know in England, and perhaps that's why, when I think about London, I can't help thinking about Brighton too, the only other place I know in England, because the Isle of Wight is now far over the sea and doesn't seem the same country, like part of the same city, like London's beach. Perhaps London, the same city that seemed to swallow you up in recent weeks, always reaches where we want it to reach. And that, to the south, can be Croydon, or Brighton. At times, when I think about London (and lately I've thought a great deal, I've thought about all its parts and about what might be the place where London swallowed you up), the city's southern limit might be in Miou.

It was autumn and it was raining. In London, it also rains a lot; it's something that people here always like to bring up in conversations, as if they were apologising but at the same time were proud of their rain, but you and I know that the rain in London is quite different to the rain in Veiga. You were coming back from Miou. You had gone to see those relatives of yours there because now you were sixteen and had to attend to family engagements. Your grandmother was getting on a bit and your mother didn't have time to attend to all of them when she appeared in

Veiga on a fortnight's holiday (or not even that). They gave you something to eat and it grew late, because in Veiga in autumn it gets dark quite early, but not like here, where there are December days when night falls well and truly before four in the afternoon, but there is a period when there is a clear lack of light.

I found you by Valín's Well. You were sat on the edge, with your right ankle resting on your left leg, washing it with a look of disgust. I didn't recognise you at first. I went over to you because I would've gone over to anyone who I saw having problems at that time and in that place, but it wasn't until the last moment that I recognised you, and even so, I didn't remember your name at first. When I did remember, I had reached you, and had asked you if something was wrong. Then I remembered that the granddaughter of the Barreses' Amalia, the daughter of Teresa, who was doing domestic work in Bilbao, was called Elisa.

You raised your head and looked towards me, your wet hair, the pain and, above all, anger in your eyes.

'I broke a heel,' you said in a faltering voice, as if you had just been crying. 'I broke my heel and then twisted my ankle.'

I don't know if you had recognised me then, if you knew that you were talking to the cobbler and that's why you mentioned the heel. In your family, you normally went to another cobbler in Veiga, Nemesio. But I came over to look, even though I knew that without my tools there wasn't much I could do. The shoe was black, a brogue, with a four- or five-centimetre heel that must have gradually weakened over time and that you had lost for good coming down the narrow pass from Miou. That was the kind of shoe that the young ladies wear on Sundays; Valentina had a pair of those, and I fixed them once. Later, when you were telling me everything, you said that you had bought them with the first wages from the stationery shop. They weren't shoes for going to see some relatives on a normal visit in the week, but you knew that those people from Miou had never looked well on your grandmother for marrying who she had married, nor your mother for getting pregnant out of wedlock, and they were always foretelling your downfall, anticipating the moment when you would call at their door in search of charity, and that's why that Thursday you were wearing those shoes.

I wasn't wrong: without my toolbox, there was little I could do to attach the heel back onto the rest of the shoe. But I suggested that you should rest your injured foot on the ground so at least we could check that it wasn't hurting so much. It was just the surprise, the anger, the rain, the fatigue. Resting on the ground, your foot no longer hurt so much. Fifteen or twenty minutes later, you were even able to continue on your way. We went slowly. That was all the severed heel allowed and the road with its puddles didn't encourage going barefoot. We were going to reach Veiga quite late; night had already fallen and there was nobody about. In London that never happens: there is always a streetlight, a house, a car to come and tear through the darkness as soon as it forms. Never in London, never, did I see darkness like that autumn evening coming back from Miou. I was going to arrive late for dinner. Inés would be worried; she didn't know that I'd left that afternoon. She must have been thinking that I was still at the cobblers and it was true that I could go out for a walk every evening I wanted. Inés didn't know a thing. I hadn't told her the business was going bad so that she wouldn't worry. But that evening perhaps she would end up finding out everything.

I don't know when it stopped bothering me that it was

raining, and that I would be late for dinner, and that Inés might discover everything. In that moment, as we went down, you kept talking. At the beginning, you were busy taking shelter in your really light coat, and drying your hair with your headscarf for the rain to make it wet it again, and trying to walk on just one heel. And you were quiet. But then all that was left behind and you started talking. It was then when you told me about your relatives in Miou. And, when you finished, you asked me what the hell I was doing around there, walking one autumn Thursday evening if I didn't have relatives to visit.

I had been going up those roads for a walk in lost moments for almost ten years, always when it was getting dark, always when I calculated that I would come across fewer people I knew. When I got married, at the start, I stopped doing it. It was like a children's game, I told myself. But two or three years ago I started going again. I would leave the old station and follow the old railway line, the one no longer in use, until my feet could not go on. Then I would go down, almost always along the road. Sometimes months went by without me going. Others, I would go two, three four days a week. I never told her why I did it, because nobody knew that I went walking along the old track. And I often thought about what excuse I would come up with if some day she asked me. But when you did, I didn't hesitate to tell you anything but the truth.

You didn't know the whole story. You had been born when the worst was over, the same year when the engineers finally worked out how to bore into a mountain, and had built a tunnel, and made the railway line go through there, and we all abandoned the old line. The same line that for years had taken my mother and me twice a month to Pontenova. Sometimes Román, my cousin, came with us too (although he didn't need to be involved in those things, from time to time he came to lend my mother a hand), but I didn't like that at all, because Román was a man by then and I didn't like it when my mother held my hand in front of him when the Civil Guard got on the train, and he was a lot less patient than she was; he soon pestered me to hurry up. But my mother seemed to like him coming with us, because that way she didn't have to enter that dark and wet basement alone, nor talk alone with that man with a harsh voice who was missing an eye and, above all, she seemed a lot more at ease on the return journey, which we always made on foot, even though it took us three or four hours, because taking the train was too risky. Sometimes, when we went with my cousin Román, she would even smile as we made our way back to Veiga.

After the war ended in Europe, the rumour began to go around that help was going to come from America, they built the new railway and you were born. We stopped going twice a month to Pontenova. And, later on, Mum died. That was when I took to walking up the old railway line, when there were no longer trains or Civil Guards or sacks of tobacco leaves or men with a harsh voice missing an eye, or cousins who would pester me, because as you know Román left Veiga at that time. And, as the cobblers began to lose customers (because now people bought shoes in shops and had more money to get new ones when the old ones were no longer any use), I would go up the railway line every week, sometimes even two evenings.

I told you all this almost without stopping for breath, without letting you reply. As soon as I shut my mouth, I felt a fool. You were very young. When you were born, the old railway line was already closed, and you never took the new one except to go and see relatives, to take your exams for the baccalaureate you never finished, to go to the doctor. You wouldn't understand the fear felt by my mother, who you hardly got to know, or my shame. I thought that you wouldn't understand anything, that you would nod out of politeness and then subtly change the subject. Or, even worse, that you would listen to the story and then go around Veiga telling everyone. *Gelo goes walking on his own in the countryside, Gelo goes walking on his own in the countryside, watch out!* Back then I didn't know you. I didn't remember your name or know who you were until the well, until I spoke to you. You were Teresa's daughter, Amalia's granddaughter. I didn't know anything else about you.

You nodded and said nothing, not out of politeness, but as if you were chewing over my words, tying up the ends of a story that I myself hadn't dared to. And then you spoke to me about you, your mother, and how you would like it if she went on the train with you and held your hand. And then I spoke again, and then you. I don't remember the last time I had spoken so much and for so long with anyone. Not with Inés.

That night nothing happened. Any one of your friends from the Women's Section, all prim and proper and full of themselves, careful to measure every word or every gesture that deviated from the doctrine, would say that nothing happened; and girls like Liz and Lydia here in London would say the same thing when one of them tells the other, at work or university, about the amorous adventures of the night before, *we didn't do anything, just talking*. We just talked. We talked and, when we got to the main road, still far from the nearest houses, where we had to go our separate ways, I leant towards you. I wasn't thinking. You drew away.

'I have to go,' you said, and off you went.

Then, on other days, we did let things happen. But I remember above all the conversations. Were you ever on the bus or train here, or waiting in the queue at the bank or Revenue and Customs, and you discover that the person stood next to you is also from Galicia, and you get talking to them, and even go and have a drink together, and it's a person you wouldn't bother with in Veiga, but here, you do, because they're right beside you, at that time and place, and speaking your language? The Italians do it with the Italians, the Greeks with the Greeks, the Indians amongst themselves, the Jamaicans. We do it too, us Galicians do it too. And you and me, too. In Veiga, we were two outsiders. And when we bumped into each other, we couldn't stop talking, talking our language. In the stationery shop they didn't speak your language. Nor did they speak it in the school you left at fourteen, three terms into the baccalaureate, and they didn't even speak it in the Women's Section which your friend Lidia was so good at disappearing into. Your mother and grandmother didn't speak it either, in spite of how much that hurt you. And that's how we would speak in the back room of the cobblers: like two outsiders who, in a foreign city, end up discovering they speak the same language. And the combat of our bodies was like that too.

That's why when you came to Croydon, when I saw you crying for the first time since we saw each other in London, I couldn't reject you at the beginning, because I thought that here, more than anywhere else, we were still two outsiders. But I regretted it afterwards. We don't talk like we used to. Nothing else is the same either.

In Veiga, we were both outsiders.

But in London you no longer are, and I still am.

Westminster

1972 went by without incident. I can only remember a quiet and easy-going year like the one back in the mid-fifties in Veiga, when I was in the middle of my twenties, and also that oppressive hunger that nobody understood (only you understood it, years later, and perhaps you, unknowingly, were undergoing a similar hunger) from my childhood and early teens. In '53 we got married and '55 and '56 and even '57 were awaiting a child although it wasn't painful: Inés and I still believed that it would happen when we least expected: '55 was also when my father-in-law retired, when he saw that I was now mastering the trade and he could quietly disappear from the scene, content that nothing would deviate from the plan that he had sketched out one day. Yes, that 1972 in London was turning out very similar to the '55 or '56 in Veiga. It was strange that London suddenly seemed like Veiga. At times, I even began to feel the hope that one day Rita would come and tell me she was pregnant. I began to think that a child, a real family, was what we needed to complete those peaceful years. But Rita never came to me with news, and neither can it be said that I found it difficult to resign myself to that.

Now we're at the end of 1973; I'm at the point of losing my job in Croydon because Mr Stobart now struggles to keep The Two Roses open (my relatives in Veiga don't believe that these things can happen in London, and secretly think that it's my fault for being lazy or dozy) because of this strange outbreak that everyone tends to call oil crisis and which I don't understand very well, with you in a place where I had never imagined you being.

When I think of how quiet 1972 ended up being, it seems almost impossible. But '72 was very quiet, of course, and I even ended up feeling a little English too.

At the beginning of February, and after many vague promises and *castles in Spain*, Tino told me that we could now start thinking seriously about opening that restaurant that had drawn me to London in the very beginning. I received the news with scepticism, but at my friend's insistence (unusual, even for him), I agreed to sit down with him one Sunday in the lounge and do sums, estimate what we had and what we needed, where would be the best area of Croydon to get established (without any nonsense this time that would turn out to be a scam, as had happened to Tino once already with some premises), how we would split the work and profits. I had to acknowledge that this time my friend was right. He had exaggerated a little, like he always did, but by my calculations, it was likely that in a year and a half or two we would have got the project off the ground. It was a considerable period of time, yes, but at least now we had set somewhere on the horizon that for the previous five years had been little more than a flight of fancy. The following week, Tino and I went to see an *accountant* who kindly explained to us what we would now have to start think about doing. To see our calculations validated by a gentleman from Croydon, and what's more a *chartered accountant*, made me think that maybe I was now beginning to think a little bit like the English.

The truth was I found myself thinking like them about other matters, not just this one, especially when I recalled my life in Veiga. Sometimes I took to thinking about Valentina, the unexpected guest in London, although not the only one, because I remember at least three more guests, and others who perhaps I never ended up finding anything about, but it was only with Valentina that you told me that thing about how all women are your sisters (and is there more truth in that word than I realised at first? I remember your mother becoming pregnant shortly after the teacher arrived in Veiga, and then he met Valentina's mother, and the girl was born, but I don't know: I don't even know what you know). When Valentina came to mind, I imagined that she would still be a teacher and also instructor in the Women's Section, maybe married by now, and I imagined what her husband would say if he knew about that visit his wife made to London, and I was surprised to think that if I were in his place, it wouldn't bother me so much. Because in England, in London, these things are done, as they are done everywhere, but no Civil Guard can come and arrest you for that, and they are done in hospitals and with a doctor and with nurses (that's what I imagined: I had never set foot in a hospital in either place, but I liked to think that that is what it's like), and not by the first old girl down a backstreet who offers to do the job for a few bob. Gelo from Veiga would never think like that; that was the business of Gelo from Croydon, who like all the English (or that's what the people from Veiga said, what my relatives from Fondrigo said when I went to see them recently) had lost his morals. I also thought about myself as a child and a lad, and I didn't understand myself, I didn't understand that misdirected anger, that hunger for I don't know what, and I thought that the little English Gelo, if he existed, wouldn't know anything about those feelings. At most, he would feel some vague, undefined anger towards the Germans (the English still look badly upon the Germans almost thirty years later, that's very clear) but nothing that would keep him awake at night.

It was a little difficult for me to tell Rita that at last

Tino and I were going to open the restaurant. Over the years, she had heard things here and there (if nothing else, she had to know why her husband was saving almost everything he earnt so devotedly), but she had never taken too much interest in the idea. Knowing Tino as she knew him from their fleeting relationship just after arriving in England, she also thought, like me, that his fantasies would never amount to anything. However, when I told her that in less than two years they could be working and that I would like – we both would like – her to join us as a cook (given that we didn't know a better cook in Croydon, or even in all London), she agreed, almost enthusiastically, if that is possible in a person as unexpressive as she was.

The life that you were living at the same time must have been a lot less quieter with work and the union and the university and the actions with Gail; but for me, from outside, it also gave me the impression of placidity that seemed to settle over all of 1972 in London. It seemed to me that you had found the road you wanted to follow and were not prepared for anything (including the exhaustion that you must have experienced) to distract you from it. That year, after much insistence (remember?), you managed to get me to find you some premises for a women's assembly (as you called it) in Croydon and perhaps to promote from there a group of women in the town, which until then had remained rigorously on the edge of Women's Liberation. The assembly was held in the Church Our Lady of Reparation building; that's why you and Gail, who introduced yourselves as speakers, had to keep your agenda to the normal and inoffensive topics: educational opportunities for women, women in the working world or (and that now began to be slightly excessive) the distribution of tasks in the home. I drank a

cup of tea (after so many years, I still don't like tea, unlike
you, but it was what the sacristan offered me) in the hall
during the assembly, reserved for women (Rita did
attend), and I could observe, curiously and even with
some pleasure, how Gail and you said goodbye to the
women in the doorway of the premises before the inquisi-
tive gaze of the priest (we know that the priests of London
are not like those in Veiga, but even so…), and afterwards, in a resounding and well-calculated guerrilla
action, you swarmed out, intercepted them a few metres
from the door and slipped something into their hands
that I couldn't make out but which were, according to
what Rita later told me, contraceptive pills, lists of med-
ical practises where they could get the pill on prescrip-
tion, and information leaflets about clinics like that one
where you took Valentina so long ago before. Many
women stood looking disconcertedly at all that and then
at both of you. But you had become a soldier, and you
were not going to let yourself be discouraged, not even by
the lack of understanding or indifference of the very people who you sought to redeem.

You kept me informed about the actions of your
women's group; like the first days in the union, I had once
gone to see you protest at the Houses of Parliament without saying anything to Rita. Surprised, right? I don't know
why I had the urge to hide that I found what you were
doing interesting, even though I didn't understand it very
well, that I wanted to be there to be sure, at least, that
your passion didn't cause you any problems. Shouting and
singing there, making up slogans on the spot, waving ban-
ners, even chaining yourself at one point to the railings at
the entrance: the impression you gave was certainly not
one of calm. But afterwards, you looked at the watch (I
was observing you from afar, always safe from being dis-

covered) and quickly composed yourself and ran off to catch the bus to do a cleaning shift or to attend a lecture in which they were going to talk to you about *Welfare policies*. As if the unrestrained Elisa who was shouting was just one more of the Elisas who worked carefully towards something that I was unaware of. In the union, you had been fighting for a wage increase of two and a half pounds, and you had achieved it: some cleaners, the *lowest of the low*, the women who cleaned up the filth of the bankers and lawyers and financiers, the men who managed a country that was heavy and difficult to manage like a warship. I couldn't image what you were now fighting for or what you might achieve.

In October 1972, you told me that I was going to see you less often from then on: perhaps the second year of university was harder than the first and you had to spend more time studying. And so it was. I only saw you three times before Christmas, twice between Christmas and Easter (when 1973 still seemed like a prolonging of the placid 1972 and Tino was doing a deal with the owner of a premises in East Croydon which, this time at last, seemed to have what we were looking for), and once in spring. And then you disappeared.

I took a week to start worrying. Not seeing you on Sundays in Portobello Road had become the norm, engrossed as you were in your studies and women's group and work. But some weeks later I realised that, if I had always had news about you before (because you would call me to notify me of some action, because Nela, who you were still visiting every two weeks at her house in Willesden Green, or Marta and Dolores, would talk to me about you, in spite of everything they were still your work colleagues, albeit sporadically: sometimes, even because I saw you in the newspaper photographed in the middle of your women's group during one especially violent protest), this time that wasn't the case. Marta and Dolores, as was expected, couldn't tell me anything. I didn't want to ask Nela; I didn't exactly know why. With Nela, London, which was never benign with anyone, had proved itself to be tougher than with everyone else. The deterioration in her sight which had started when she was still young and mended trousers advanced almost uncontrollably, cleaning had punished her back and knees, and now, what's more (they said), her mind was being swept away. I didn't know how Nela would respond if I just asked her about Elisa. For an entire afternoon in Portobello Road, I went after Lidia, who simply had to know something (if there was anything to know) from her mother, but the girl (who had been your best friend when you two had set foot in London) replied evasively and hardly trying to hide it. And then I couldn't worry anymore, because Rita insisted that we had to go to Coruña that year, as a new nephew had been born and she wanted to see him, and we spent a month there.

Had she done it on purpose? I don't know, Elisa. I know the devotion, of Rita's approach to her nephews and nieces, and I don't dare to disagree with her regarding anything to do with them. I thought that perhaps they were like children for her, the children we never had, we don't have, and I didn't dare say a thing. So, I went to the travel agent, bought the plane tickets and kept them in the drawer of the bedside table until the day we left. One month. I think that I had never been away from London for so long, and although Coruña is not Veiga either, I settled in easily as if in my own home. And in this home of mine there was no space for you, it hurts me to say. Did she do it on purpose? Did Rita do the same that Inés had done so many years ago: take me through insinuations, half words, to an intimate, protected space of our own, a space in which you didn't fit? I don't know, Elisa. Of course, if she did it on purpose, she succeeded. It hurts me even more to say that in the time I spent in Coruña, amongst nephews and nieces, parties and relatives, I stopped thinking about you and your absence. I only remembered the two days that I was in Veiga. I went to sort out the matter of an inheritance with some relatives from Fondrigo. And there I thought about you again. Actually, I didn't remember until I thought I saw your grandmother from afar, on the other side of the Acerón. Then they told me that it wasn't her, but it was enough for you to come back into my head. For a moment, I even began to play with the idea that you yourself might be in Veiga, far from the City and the union and Women's Lib and the university and Gail, far from everything that fed you through those roots that you had planted beneath the pavements of London. I know that in five years you never returned to Veiga. I also know that you never stopped writing to your grandmother or your mother. I thought about all that as I returned that day to the house in Fondrigo, after seeing that woman I mistook for Amalia. But two days later I returned to Coruña, and I forgot about you again.

When I got back, you came into my memory again. We still hadn't left Heathrow Airport (you don't know it; you came here by ferry from Santander, as I did the first time, and then you never left) and I was already thinking about you, about the Elisa who was missing in that city to which I had just returned. Rita noticed that I wasn't listening to her, that I was replying to her questions in a routine way, that I was blank, and asked me what the matter was. I replied that I was feeling sick and she stopped asking me. So, as we returned to Croydon by train, I could think about you and where you would be. And it was then when I checked Portobello Road, the first time I saw you, where I met the English Elisa. And Willesden Green, where everything began. And Oxford Street and Brighton and Hampstead and the City and Bethnal Green. And Westminster. And Croydon. And Miou, Miou too.

The next day was Sunday. That meant a dance, and Portobello Road, and perhaps seeing Lidia and daring to ask her about you again. Rita didn't understand that I wanted to go to the dance, above all when we came back from spending a month in Coruña, at the same Galician dances and outings that the bar in Portobello Road tried to imitate. In the end, I went alone. Lidia was on the floor, dancing with some lad who was at least five years younger than her, although Lidia seemed to have made a pact with the devil the day she arrived in London: moving on the dance floor, with her deliberately languid and uncoordinated arms, with her half-closed eyelashes, she resembled a seductive and inoffensive doll, *harmless and tasteless*. I made my way to her through the dancers, and without further ado, asked her:

'Where's Elisa?'

She shrugged her shoulders in a gesture between innocent and disparaging, without stopping dancing. Her companion instinctively drew closer to her, creating at the same time a barrier between her and me. It was clear that he didn't like that approach to his friend. I turned around and spent the rest of the evening at the bar, waiting for a more favourable moment that never came along.

Today it's Sunday again. Today it's three months since the last time I had news of you, the last time I spoke to you in this same place. *Come back, baby, come back*, play the speakers behind me: one of those ironies that the

English enjoy so much. Today, Lidia is dancing in front of me again, but this time alone: her companion is nowhere to be seen. I look around me, in search of faces I know that might dissuade me, I look at Lidia, I look at the floor, I think about the things I never wanted to think about. And I move towards Lidia and this time press her hand firmly against her shoulder so that she stops dancing and looks at me, and I ask her the same question.

'I don't know,' Lidia shouts above the music.

'Yes, you do,' I reply. I do know that although your relationship with Lidia isn't what it used to be, there's no way that you wouldn't tell your news to Nela, your London mother, one of your mothers from here together with Gail.

'Let's get out of here. Buy me a drink in the Brazilians' pub,' Lidia finally says, making her way between the dancers who crowd the floor. I don't know how I convinced her. Perhaps my look was more menacing than the week before, or more pleading. Perhaps (I never found out) you yourself gave Lidia instructions to reveal only when you want where you are and what fate London had in store for you.

In the Brazilians' pub, which is almost door to door with the bar, Lidia lowers her voice, even though nobody knows us in there.

'I heard this from my mum,' she makes clear before starting, 'because Elisa is still very fond of her and hates to cause her needless worry. If it weren't for her, she wouldn't tell me anything either. It's been a while since she did. Since Jim, or even before that.'

So, then I hear from Lidia's mouth what seems to be the most beautiful story I ever heard. Because it ends well, like all films, books and stories should. Because it ends with you still alive. I find out that they arrested you three months earlier outside Parliament. Everything began with one of those demonstrations that you, Gail (although Gail wasn't at that particular one) and your group organise on a regular basis, one of the many that I knew nothing about, because you were very active and it didn't escape me that you preferred to hide some of your actions from me. The police where there, but of course they always were and they always left you more or less alone. You had been demonstrating a good while and protesting when one of the policemen went over to the group and told you that the slogan you were shouting at that moment was technically an obscenity. Perhaps you would like to shout something else, he suggested. English police are different; English police always suggest, they never order. That was nothing new for you, either. You had already complained to me more than once that the English like very much to classify certain things as obscenity, but afterwards they didn't do anything about it. So you continued to shout, and the others followed. The policeman went over to you again. It was clear that he was a little fed up (perhaps he hadn't slept well the night before, or didn't particularly sympathise with the cause of Women's Liberation), and didn't treat you with the courtesy that is normally the case with the British police. You flared up too, brandishing the banner that you were carrying and planted it in his face. The truth is that you didn't want to do anything to him, you didn't even want to touch him, you just wanted him to see the banner up close and for him to know that you women were not going to back down so easily. But you went too far and poked him in the eye with one of the corners of the banner. The man ended up in hospital. And you, in the police station.

'They didn't hold her very long, just one night,' Lidia

explained, as if she were in Veiga chattering about the love life of someone or other instead of telling me about the confrontation between a friend of hers, or former friend of hers, and no less than the London Metropolitan Police. 'They decided she didn't pose any danger and released her until the hearing. She could go home, to work, university, wherever she wanted. But Gail said it was better if she didn't go around there much, to not set things off again, wind up another policeman and end up even worse off. So she took her to her house. She spends the day indoors, maybe reading and preparing more non-sense that perhaps they'll get up to when all this is over. They say Gail has a friend who is a lawyer and she's pulling strings so that she doesn't go to prison.'

'Can I go and see her?' I ask. At first, I could hardly speak with the joy of knowing that she was alright, that she was alive. But then I start thinking that in this country I'm an outsider, you're an outsider and we all know that although the rest of the country might be friendly and patient and understanding, in any country, outsiders don't tend to get on very well with the police or judges, or vice-versa.

'No,' Lidia interrupted. 'Gail doesn't want anyone, they don't want anyone. After a lot of insisting, my mum managed to persuade her to let her go to the hearing. I'll go with her, I've no choice, because you know that my mum hardly speaks English and she wouldn't cope some-where like that.'

Then I get serious. I don't know what might happen to someone in England who disobeys a policeman. England isn't Veiga, I repeat to myself. 1973, that year which until that moment has been so placid, is not 1936. And a policeman, and much less a bobby, is not a mayor, or a priest, or a sergeant in the Civil Guard. And you're not my father. I repeat it again and again to myself. I look at Lidia, as if expecting her to say that it will all be alright, that in England all these things are not so important, that everybody knows that this is a barbaric land and nothing works the same way as in Veiga, but Lidia doesn't say anything. She finishes her bottle of beer, lights a cigarette and gets up without saying goodbye.

I won't tell you how I spent the twenty-three days that were left until the hearing. I never felt less from here, I never preferred so much to have stayed in Veiga and for you to have stayed there too, where the punishment for poking a policeman's eye out was certainly severe, but where to confront a policeman would be above all a possibility that neither you or I would dare even think about. It's Tuesday and I'm working at The Two Roses on the lunchtime shift, but on Sunday I saw Lidia in Portobello Road and asked her to call me here when she had news. I don't know if she will, but, when I'm folding my waistcoat and taking off my bow tie, Mrs Stobart appears and tells me I have a call. It's clear that the woman is dying of curiosity (I never get calls at the restaurant), but she's too English to stay standing there beside me when I pick up the earpiece and sit down looking at a corner, turning my back to her without worrying about manners.

'Hello, Lidia'

And then I find out that you, after a month of almost seclusion, made a triumphant entry in the City of Westminster court in Victoria, accompanied by Millicent (Gail's lawyer friend), Gail and various women from your group. Lidia felt ashamed (and it was noticeable through the earpiece of the telephone: it was as if her voice were red with shame) that the judge or the lawyers or the court officials might think that she or her mother had something to do with that bunch of lunatics, and that's why

Nela sat on one of the benches at the back, well away
from the others, although that meant that she didn't
understand half of what was going on at the hearing. You
didn't stop smiling during the entire hearing, as if you
were defying the judge, and the one-eyed policeman
(who also attended as a member of the public and sat in
the second row) and all England, which at first had welcomed you only for you to rebel against it, was sat there,
in the City of Westminster court, to judge you. They listened to each other and then the judge said that he found
you guilty of involuntary aggression and obscenity and
that he was sentencing you to a year in prison for the first
offence and two months for the second. Then you, who
had until then been very quiet except for a mocking smile
that you wore painted on your face from the moment you
came through the door, stood up and began to shout that
you admitted and recognised the aggression, but not the
obscenity and how could that man dare to condemn you
for obscenity when each day thousands of obscenities are
said and committed against women without any judge
condemning any man for that. The other women stood
up too and joined in (they seemed to really enjoy themselves, Lidia pointed out, including Gail, although she
remained seated and silent), and Millicent, the lawyer,
covered her head with her hands. The judge struggled to
maintain order, threatened to charge you for contempt of
court too, and threatened to charge all of you. That a
young woman, in addition to being a guest of the country,
should display this type of behaviour was, he said quite
seriously, simply *appalling*. Finally, everyone was quiet,
including you, and when the sentence was read, nothing
more was said. Fourteen months in Holloway Prison.
Millicent, Lidia comments, seemed quite satisfied. With
all the testimonies that were given, it was ridiculous to

think that you could be acquitted, and anyway, the final scene with the judge made her nervous: she would be happy if the two of you had got out of their alive. She put her hands on your shoulders and took you out of the room as quickly as she could, both of you escorted by Gail and the rest of the women. In a few seconds, only Nela and Lidia were left in the court room, still asking themselves if that was still England, the greyish, quiet and very civilised country that had welcomed them years before.

I hang up the telephone, quite satisfied. I am satisfied. You're not going to die, like my dad died many years ago, the day when the country in which he was born became a foreign land to him overnight. Fourteen months in Holloway Prison, but you're going to live. London, luckily, doesn't seem to ask much of those who have to redeem their offences towards it. Fourteen months. An infernal winter, a timid spring, a period on the beach in Brighton that gradually draws to a close until fading into another winter, and missing out on that in prison is not important, because it's ugly and inhospitable anyway and turns your home into a prison cell. That's all your fourteen months in Holloway Prison are going to be, in the Holloway district, in the north of the city. They're just going to be a few months, fourteen months, and you and I, the two of us, know that in London that doesn't amount to anything.

Holloway

Visits are on Monday afternoon. I found out because Nela told me: she's been twice. Lidia went with her to the door and spoke to the staff on her behalf, because Nela hasn't learnt English in five years and won't learn now, but Lidia waits outside, smoking; she never went in and never will. Gail went and Millicent, of course, was your most regular visitor. But I'm going to be the first man to visit you. Two weeks ago, I asked Mr Stobart to let me have this Monday free (and it wasn't difficult for him, because it's Christmas, and at Christmas it's always quieter at the restaurant). I took the train from East Croydon to Victoria and then the Tube to Piccadilly. It snowed yesterday. In these five years I've been in London, I never saw it snow more than two or three days every winter, and seeing the streets and rooftops and the chimneys covered in white is always a strange and childlike celebration and today, in spite of everything, it was just that. In prison, however, everything is grey, but clear grey, almost white, and the staff limit themselves to asking for the papers that I brought and to check names and dates in silence: they don't ask me any question that might startle me; they don't seem like prison officers. They were just surprised a little, the same as all the English, to meet a man called Ángel, angel, *Ayn-gell*. And as I move towards the corridor behind some of these such benevolent warders, I think that this is more like a hospital than a prison.

They take me to a room painted white, bare, divided in two by a line of tables and chairs. They tell me to sit down at one of the free places. It's now one of the few left: you can tell it's almost Christmas. And soon you appear.

You're wearing a grey outfit made of ordinary fabric, shapeless and without frills. You don't look like a prisoner: in fact, dressed like that, you don't look much different to Rita when she puts on one of those really English outfits that she was given by Mrs Raymond. If this were a hospital, you could easily be a nurse. A nurse. Remember? What you wanted to be when you met Jim and began to go to English class in West Hampstead, so long ago. A nurse or a patient who spent a long time in isolation with tuberculosis, or with pneumonia, and who is now on the verge of recovery and whose cheeks are rosy and full (you're not thinner than the last time I saw you, right?), but whose eyes still shine with the recollection of the temperature and your ankles are still not strong enough. But you are smiling.

'Here I am,' you say to me now. Your voice sounds distorted, strange, full of echoes that are not your own. This room isn't very big, it's full of people and they all talk at once; that's why. Or perhaps after a few weeks in prison you've already picked up the Caribbean and African and Irish and London accent of your fellow prisoners.

'Are you well? Are you eating alright?' In spite of the wardens being friendly and you seeming well fed, I can't help lowering my voice and looking instinctively around me with a quick gesture.

You laugh.

'Of course. The food isn't what you serve at The Two Roses, that's for sure, but it's not so bad either. And it's just us naughty girls here, the ones they think they can put back on the right track after a few months rotting here from boredom. There are several cleaners and shop assistants who are here for stealing from their bosses. For food and clothes, most of them, but you know how judges don't get that. And some older women like those who sorted things out in the villages when young girls got pregnant and didn't have the money or the means to go to hospital. We're not a bad group. The worst thing is the boredom. There's not a lot to do here.'

We continue talking about life in Holloway and then life in Croydon. You ask me about Rita, Tino and all the people that you and I know south of the river. Then the conversation turns to prison, the visits by Millicent, Gail's lawyer friend who, according to what you tell me, is taking care of your case for free as a gesture of her commitment to the cause and who goes to see you punctually each week.

'There might be good news. Millicent thinks that I'm not going to do the fourteen months here. I just have to behave well. Be seen in the sewing room, the laundry, show them that I'm not a burden to the *community* as they say, and they'll let me out two or three months early. So, I won't spend next Christmas stuck in here.

'So, what are you going to do?'

You shrug your shoulders.

'I don't know. I told Millicent that I wanted to stay here, finish my university studies and became a social worker, like I told you. But she's not at all optimistic. She told me that there's no social worker job that doesn't require a criminal record certificate. That's normal, because they work closely with the police and no borough is going to want a social worker who leaves a *bobbie* almost blind' (at that moment, you laugh at your own words, and I laugh with you). 'She suggested I might go for something else, something like office work, because they're not going to want me as a teacher or nurse, either. Or that, or go back to cleaning. But I don't want to.'

'So?'

Now you take a while to answer.

'I might go back to Veiga. I could write to my mum, tell her that she can go back too and that this time we're going to open the haberdashery. That would make her happy.'

'Are you being serious?' I ask. I don't believe that you would want to go back to Veiga; you're English now, in Veiga you'd be a foreigner, like I am here, like we all are. Or maybe, in the time I haven't seen you, something happened that made you English and from Veiga at the same time, from everywhere in the world where there are women, cleaners, foreigners, where there are people who suffer and cry.

'Yes. Veiga. My grandmother. My mum. I never told you, but here in London I always missed them. I've still got a lot of months left inside here to think it over.'

A bell rings. The other prisoners, their visitors, even the women guards who watch you from a distance like sphinxes, seem to instinctively stir. Visiting time is over.

'Now I have to go,' you say, as if apologising, 'Come back and see me, okay? If not, I might die. Of boredom.'

Then, for the first time during the visit, you stretch out your hand to brush mine. And I feel warmth, first on my hand, then all my body afterwards, that same warmth in Veiga when you interlocked your fingers with mine in the very moment when we managed to be alone in the shoe shop. It's the same warmth. I raise my head. It's the same warmth, but then it seems like another woman. I see that in prison you let your hair grow really long, and now it's all tangled up, and your face is almost completely framed by white hair that now threatens to spread mercilessly across the rest of your brown mane. You're just twenty-eight, but now I remember, Teresa went grey quickly too, and I remember her a little older than what you are now with her braids already grey; the women in your family, the Barreses, go grey quickly. And your dark eyes are starting to cross, and that gaze once so firm is now asymmetric and full of shadows. And this time I remember that your grandmother Amalia used to go cross-eyed behind her glasses. You never looked like Teresa, you never looked like Amalia. I always thought, even though I never told you, that you must look like your father, whoever he was, but in Holloway Prison I notice, for the first time, the mark left on you by your mother and grandmother. The one that can be seen and the one that cannot.

And you seem to read my mind.

'Don't say anything to them,' you ask me as you get up. The female guard comes over to you from behind and reminds us, in a gruff and indifferent voice, that *Time is up*. 'My mother and my grandmother don't know I'm here. They don't know a thing. They think that I'm still cleaning and studying whenever I can. But don't say anything to them. I'll write to them when I find the way of telling them.'

'*Time is up*,' the warder says again, almost shouting, with that sour voice of hers. We're now the last ones left in the room. The rest of the visitors were more obedient, more English, and finished their visit on time as soon as the bell rang.

'I have to go,' you say, brushing my hand.

I feel a warmth again that gradually fades as you go through the room escorted by the gruff-voiced guard. First you are Elisa from behind, with your hair loose and a grey outfit, then you are a slim woman of indeterminate identity, then, before disappearing definitively through the door that leads back to the prison, a tiny grey dot in the middle of an immense city, of an immense and somewhat grey and a slightly white world, like the old hair framing your face and, as I am now seeing, on the nape of your neck too, sliding down your back. I wait until the door closes and then get to up make my way back to Croydon in the London that is slowly being covered by snow.